A DREAM OF DEMOCRACY

My Flight, My Life — Helmut Siewert

D0898317

Helmut Siewert, Dieter Siewert, Marlene Siewert

A DREAM OF DEMOCRACY

My Flight, My Life — Helmut Siewert

a novel based on a

True Story of WWII

Helmut Siewert &

Cheryl Bartlam du Bois

A Place In Time.Press Beverly Hills, CA

A Place in Time.Press
8594 Wilshire Blvd. Ste. 1020,
Beverly Hills, CA 90211
310 613-8872

e-mail: info@aplaceintime.press

Website: aplaceintime.press

Cover Design & Layout: Christopher Staser, brandweaver.tv
Map Design & Illustration: Steve Luchsinger

Library of Congress Cataloging-in-Publication Data is available on file.

Print ISBN: 978-0-9745414-2-6
Ebook ISBN: 978-0-9745414-3-3

Historical Fiction

Printed in the United States of America

Our books may be purchased in bulk for promotional, educational, or business use. Please contact your local bookseller or the publisher.

First U.S. Edition 2022

TABLE OF CONTENTS

PART II: ESCAPING COMMUNISIM
1952 – 1954 West Germany

PART III: A DREAM OF A NEW LIFE
1954 – 2021   New York — Wisconsin — Florida, USA

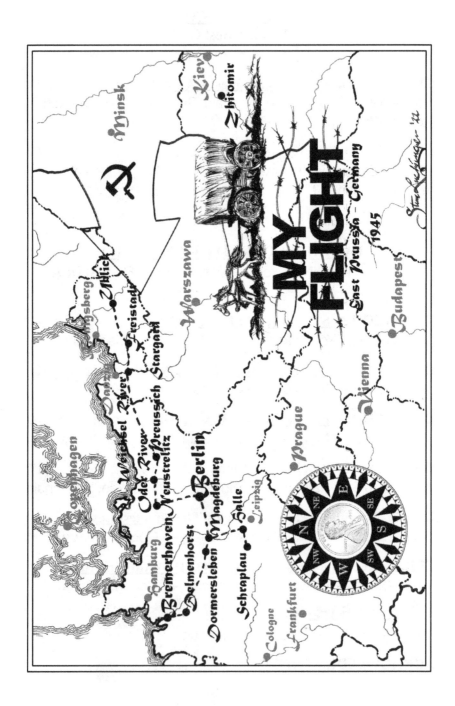

MY FLIGHT

East Prussia – Germany

1945

PART I

ESCAPING THE RED ARMY

JANUARY 5, 1945 – 1954 — West Prussia/Westpreußen,
Germany — East Prussia/Osteprußen, Germany

PROLOGUE

<u>The Russian Invasion</u>

January 1945 — WWII — Germany

It was the last breath of World War II. Hitler's generals knew after the first day of the Russian offensive, with the German army's extensive losses of armor and artillery not to mention men, that they had in effect lost the war on the Eastern Front.

Helmut Siewert, halfway through his tenth year, six of which had been spent as a young boy growing up in the midst of one of the world's most vicious wars, was living a modest life with his mother, Lydia, and five-year-old sister, Marlene. The family owned a small five-family building in the town of Bischofswerder in West Prussia. Despite a chronic leg injury, Helmut's father, Gustav, had been drafted and required to report to the German army for the second time in 1944, leaving his family alone and unprotected. Two weeks later his injury, which refused to heal, landed him in the hospital twenty kilometers away from home. The road was difficult to travel so Gustav and Lydia exchanged letters. Rather than release him, the German Army found him to be the perfect test subject for medical experiments of new drugs and forced him to stay.

By Christmas of 1944, the Russians had already crossed the German boarder northeast of Bischofswerder into Konigsberg, the capital of East Prussia, where it was rumored they were pillaging everything in their path. For the Germans, the entire front was beginning to collapse like a house of cards. There had been rumblings and promises of an orderly, planned evacuation for German civilians, due to the Red Army's German Offensive, but they had delayed the action until October 1944. By then, the Civil Services and the Nazi Party were overwhelmed by the numbers of citizens desperate to evacuate—over two million in total. Because of their poor planning and the speed of the Soviet advance, thousands of refugees were caught in the midst of combat as they fled via wagon trains to the west with only what they could carry, leaving everything else behind to be ravaged by the Russian Army.

Unfortunately, the brutality of the Russian Army had been instigated and set in stone by Hitler himself, when he viciously invaded the Soviet Union on June 22, 1941—operation Barbarossa—with Moscow, Leningrad, and Stalingrad as his goals.

The German Army eventually invaded Russia as far to the east as the Ural Mountains. Due to Hitler's belief that the Germanic race—the 'Herrenvolk' or Master Race—was far superior to all others, especially the Slavs, which he considered as subhuman he attacked the Russian Army with more vengeance and callousness than even his deadly campaign against the Poles. Hitler even deemed that the conventional moral code of the Geneva Convention, regarding the humane treatment of prisoners of war and noncombatants, was not applicable and so duly and ruthlessly annihilated all that lay in his path. As stated by his General Erich Hoepner to the Fourth Panzer Group on May 2, 1941, "….In concept and execution, each fighting engagement must be guided by an iron will to annihilate the enemy totally and without pity." And, later on October 10, 1941, Sixth Army, Field Marshal Walter von Reichenau ordered his troops as such—First—"The utter destruction of Bolshevist heresy, of the Soviet state and its war machine." Second—"The merciless extermination of foreign cunning and cruelty, thereby securing the life of the German Wehrmacht in Russia. This is the only way we can live up to our historic task of liberating the German people once and for all from the Asiatic-Jewish peril." Hitler promised the German people 'Lebensraum'/'living space'/'room for life for all.' Those who were part non-Aryan races were, subject to expulsion, or total destruction.

In essence, Hitler's severe regulations produced roving murder squads in the areas of Russia controlled by the German Army. Civilians were executed if suspected as collaborators and all political commissars were immediately put to death. The guidelines for Operation Barbarossa's troops in Russia ordered extreme measures against "Bolshevik agitators, guerrillas, saboteurs, and Jews." Any prisoners of war taken by the German Army were so inhumanely treated that the Red Army soldiers were determined to fight to their death rather than be captured and interned in a POW camp.

The German Army not only conscripted civilians to work on the front lines building fortifications and burying the dead, but it requisitioned most of the available food supplies, leaving the local population to starve. Ultimately, the German Army was stopped outside of Stalingrad, Moscow, and Leningrad. This is where Helmut's uncle, August Fester, a German soldier, was captured and imprisoned in a work camp before being marched on foot all the way to Siberia. August's wife, Elke, and twelve-year-old daughter, Ingrid, were taken as slaves and repeatedly raped.

The German Army had left behind a scorched-earth policy—burning homes, businesses, and machinery as well as poisoning all wells. Germany's Fuehrer had accomplished little other than planting the seeds for the Soviet Union and the Red Army to seek total revenge by the time they finally entered East and West

Prussia in late 1944 and early 1945. The die had been cast for its total and complete annihilation.

CHAPTER 1

<u>The Flight – Die Flucht</u>

January 5, 1945 — West Prussia, Germany

It was the middle of an icy cold January night when Lydia Siewert shook her ten-year-old son awake from a sound sleep. "Get up Helmut, we have to leave. They're coming! Get dressed. Wear your warmest clothes. Pack light, I will wake your sister!"

Helmut rubbed his eyes in the darkness and quickly leapt from his bed. Although the family and the neighbors rarely spoke of a possible Russian invasion, Helmut had been expecting this exodus from his home for nearly a year, but he had always thought that somehow the German Army would provide them time to safely escape ahead of the Russian Army, or that Germany would win the war. Now it seemed time had run out and the Red Army was upon them since he could already hear artillery and cannons in the distance.

Lydia packed two small cases with warm clothing and included family documents and nearly fire thousand marks, dressed her five-year old daughter, Marlene, and hurried her children down the stairs of their three-story building that they would have to leave, never to return. "Get the sled Helmut. We'll pull your sister and the cases through the snow."

When they stepped out in the freezing night air, other families were frantically running and shouting as they hurriedly packed to leave their homes. It was total chaos in the streets as horse-drawn wagons were already lined up moving slowly, up to two abreast, totally blocking the street. Lydia rushed to fall into the line of evacuees behind one of the wagons, dragging the heavy sled through the deep snow. Helmut ran to keep up, grabbing onto the rope of the sled to help his mother. Confusion and despair reigned in the streets with mothers struggling to push baby carriages and their small children following behind. Young boys grappled with carts full of belongings and a number of elderly men and woman walked with difficulty alongside the wagons. Many other townspeople seemed to wander aimlessly looking for loved ones.

Following behind the wagon made the sled easier to pull, however they had to be careful to avoid being trampled by the horses and wagon behind. Luckily, there were so many refugees fleeing, the wagons could go no faster than they could walk.

There were only elderly men on the wagon-train since all men between the ages of sixteen and sixty had been conscripted into the German Army, leaving only the young boys and the infirm to assist the women and children with their exodus. With the main roads blocked by the army, they were forced to stay on the icy cobblestone streets, making it even more difficult to walk. Helmut turned to his mother, "Mutti, when will we be allowed to return?"

"Take a look at your home Helmut, my dear, for it will be your last. I'm afraid you will not see it again."

Helmut shivered, more from that thought than the below-freezing temperature, which hadn't had time to seep into his bones quite yet. "Where are we going Mutti?"

"West to the train station. We'll take the train to Berlin. We have family near there that we can stay with. You know my cousin, Johann. He's been drafted, but his wife, Maria, will take us in. It will be all right."

"But what about father? How will he find us?" questioned Helmut, starting to panic. "We can't just leave without telling him!"

"Your father will find us Helmut," Lydia patted him on the back. "Rest your mind at ease, he will find us."

But the last thing that Helmut's mind felt was rested, or at ease. There were a million questions swirling around his head and they, with the icy wind that froze his nostrils as he breathed, left him dizzy. He thought they would have had more time. Time to plan their move to the west with his father before the Russians came, as had so many others. How could he have known that the fighting on the Russian front would progress so rapidly to the west? Worse yet, how could he have known that the Germans were losing their fight against the Red Army— those ruthless, vicious killers he had been warned about? He had been told stories of how the Russians hated the Nazis from when they had invaded the Soviet Union and that their ultimate goal was to rape and pillage Prussia. "Mutti….what does rape and pillage mean?"

"Where did you hear that Helmut….?! We don't talk about such things! Hush now, you'll scare your sister!"

But even at such a young age Helmut knew what it meant. He fell silent still needing answers but knowing he would get none. It was tradition in his family not to discuss questionable things, like where the Jews disappeared to since Adolph Hitler had come to power. Jews like his best friend, Jacob, who had disappeared when he was eight.

It was a dark foggy night with no stars or moon to guide them on their two-kilometer walk to the train station; however, fires burned in the distant sky from torched houses and shelling could be heard in the distance. All they could do was to follow the wagon ahead and be sure to keep up so the one behind did not run them over in the dark. Helmut's legs, in his short pants and stockings, were frozen and his arms were quite numb from pulling the sled with his mother, but he didn't want to complain. His mother was worried enough. It was an especially severe winter with bitter cold nights reaching four degrees Fahrenheit and it took the family an hour to get close to the train station. As the eastern glow started to illuminate the town ahead of them, it didn't take Lydia long to realize the vast numbers of citizens already waiting for the train, pushing and shoving in order to get to the front of the line. There was nothing organized, nor orderly, about their departure, as the Nazi Party had promised the German citizens. Hundreds lined the streets waiting for a train that was rumored to never come. They were only a few in a sea of thousands of people hoping to escape the rapidly advancing Russian Army and it was overwhelming for Helmut to comprehend. The chances of getting onboard the train before the Russians arrived boded slim odds, but Lydia kept it to herself so as not to worry Helmut. He was overly sharp for a ten-year-old and she knew he would soon figure out the predicament that their only chance of escape would likely be to walk all the way to Berlin. Since they'd sold their farm in the country, due to Gustav's poor health, they had also sold their horse and wagon, which would have greatly aided their exodus to the west.

They stood in the cold for hours waiting for the train, with no breakfast, or confirmation that the train would ever come. Lydia had assumed they would be able to buy food along the way, however with the mob of refugees it was obvious that it would be impossible to find nourishment for her children. Helmut was already sensing Lydia's feeling of helplessness as it washed over her. She tried, but could no longer hide it from showing on her face as she comforted Marlene, who cried from the cold and her hunger. By midday they still stood far from the train platform with little hope of becoming one of the passengers to make it onto the train. Surely the mob ahead of them would fill the train before they got to the front of the line, Lydia assessed. Even if the train did arrive, it was unlikely to be her best chance of getting her children to safety. Word had spread that Hitler had just given evacuation orders, but it seemed they had come more than a day too late.

"I think we should have left days ago," Helmut said matter-of-factly as he generally could assess a situation quickly.

"I am so sorry Helmut, we should not have waited. I made the mistake of believing the authorities, that they would stop the Russians at the border." Lydia stood strong in the face of hopelessness just as someone shouted her name. Lydia turned to see a wagon approaching, attempting to join the wagon train that traveled down the main street. The sun was shining brightly behind the driver, so Lydia had to shield her eyes to make out the identity of the woman calling her name from the wagon.

"Tante Auguste!" shouted Helmut waving, "Cousin Wilfried!" The wagon neared them revealing the face of the woman and her son.

"Oh Auguste! It's so good to see you," cried Lydia.

"Lydia! I was so worried about you. I didn't know how to find you. You must come with us."

"We planned to take the train to Berlin. I was afraid it would be too hard on the children to make the journey by wagon."

"There will be no trains. I've heard they are not coming. You must come with us! We have plenty of food for everyone and food for the horses. Please…. get in the wagon!"

Lydia was hesitant as she turned to look at Helmut, realizing what she would be committing her children to for weeks to come, but the alternative could be much worse. Her main concern was to protect her children from the Russians no matter what. Yet she knew the pain and suffering, as well as the danger they would be forced to bear should they go with Auguste on the wagon train across the open countryside.   But it was far better than walking.

"Mutti, I think Tante is right. There are too many people and even if the train does come we will never get on," Helmut reasoned.

Against her better judgment, Lydia quickly agreed to join them on the wagon as she lifted Marlene up to sit beside Auguste. Helmut passed up their cases and tied the sled into the back of the wagon as Lydia climbed aboard. She reached down to help Helmut up, but he refused. "That's okay, I'll walk to stay warm."

"Are you sure? You must be exhausted. Please let us know if you can't keep up, Helmut."

"I'm fine Mutti. I'd rather walk to keep my feet warm."

Since young boys Helmut's age still wore only short pants with their long woolen socks, he was quite unprepared to stay warm in the below freezing weather. Lydia passed Helmut a woolen blanket to wrap around his shoulders, but due to the open hand-knit work of his grandmother, it didn't totally shelter him from the cold, blowing winds and snow. However inadequate it was he was still grateful to have it and he thanked God that he had thought to wear his lace-up high-top boots. Navigating the snow and ice on the roads in his wooden shoes would have been impossible.

Helmut smiled up at his family in the wagon and Wilfried flicked the reins, driving the horses, Hans and Liesel, forward as they fell into line between two other wagons. They drove on at a slower pace than Helmut would have liked to walk in order to stay warm, but the road was so congested with wagons it was impossible to travel faster.

Auguste had left home that morning, hoping to meet with Lydia and her children as they had originally planned when they thought their evacuation would be an organized by the government officials. She had no way of knowing how difficult it might be to find them in such a sea of refugees, but it seemed that fate, or simply luck, had intervened and their paths crossed at the right moment, allowing Auguste to rescue Helmut and his family.

Auguste was Lydia's sister-in-law who lived a few kilometers away from her in a town called Bischofswerder, in West Prussia, with only her fourteen-and-a-half-year-old son, Wilfried, and her elderly mother-in-law, Pauline. Her sixteen-year-old son, Gerhard, as well as her husband, Johann, had been conscripted into the German Army and her daughter Irmgard worked as an army nurse, wherever needed, and was married to a German doctor.   Johann had been assigned to a prisoner of war camp for

American pilots near the Russian border, but Auguste was uncertain of the whereabouts of her son, or even if he was still alive.

They made Pauline, an eighty-five-year-old invalid, as comfortable as possible in the covered wagon, nestled into warm blankets, but Auguste quietly expressed her concerns to Lydia about her mother-in-law's condition wondering if she would survive the trip. Lydia constantly checked on Pauline and comforted her and her own daughter Marlene, who often cried from the cold and discomfort. To soothe her, Lydia would rub her daughter's face, hands, and feet to help keep her warm and ward off frostbite.

Auguste aided Wilfried in driving the team when he found it necessary to walk to help others, or to look for possible food that wasn't frozen. She had clearly prepared ahead for this event since aboard the wagon were plenty of stores, consisting of barrels of meats, sausages, and potatoes. There was only one small problem. The temperatures were so low, even during the day; their food supplies remained frozen solid. Even the bread was frozen into a solid brick making it impossible to eat, so they found it difficult to nourish themselves since they couldn't stop to build a fire to cook their meals. At least the hay and grain for the horses was still edible. Whenever they were forced to stop at intersections to allow German convoys to pass, Wilfried would hang a feedbag around the horses' necks to keep their energy up.

Since their water supply was also frozen he would give the horses and his family scoops of fresh snow to eat to quench their thirst. It was Wilfried's job to care for the horses and the wagon and Helmut helped him when he wasn't looking for food from closed shops along the way. The family's only edible food for the first few days was the frozen bread that Auguste had prepared before they left. Luckily, Wilfried had brought his hatchet, which he used to hack off bite-size pieces of frozen bread for the family to suck on until it thawed enough to eat. It would be days before they would have time to stop to make coffee from the grain and warm cooked meals to fill their bellies.

With many of the main roads blocked by the military they found it necessary to stay on the lesser-maintained roads, making the going tough for the wagons—many breaking wheels or axels and left sitting along the side of the road. Within the wagon train, the neighbors from each town were grouped together in 'trecks,' each led by a young man—their 'treck' leader. Helmut's leader was a sixteen-year-old boy from Wilfried's town named, Erich, who was responsible for the wellbeing of the fifteen families from their small town that comprised their 'treck.' It didn't take long for the wagons to be separated; however, as the forced closures and other wagons entering the train managed to cut off wagons, parting them from their friends.

By the end of the first day, they had traveled the eight-to-nine kilometers to the town of Freistadt but finding no shelter they spent the night on the wagon, either pushing forward at a snail's pace, or stopped to allow the German Army to pass. At dawn, the wagons slowly started to move again, but once they entered the town, Helmut and his family realized why they had been delayed for so long. There was a roadblock with the German Army checking papers to be certain that only German citizens, or Polish people of semi-German descent, who were not forced to wear a large 'P,' on their backs, got through. No full-blooded Poles, who wore the letter 'P,' or Jews, who wore a letter 'J,' were allowed to evacuate the area. When their wagon pulled to a stop in front of the German officers, Wilfried handed their passports and identification cards to the armed guard blocking their passage. The officer scrutinized the documents and then looked in the wagon to find Pauline and Marline sleeping under blankets. Then he stepped back to face Wilfried, who stood next to the horses holding their reins.

"This says you are fourteen and a half. You will soon be required to join the army as a helper to the soldiers."

"Yes, but I'm only fourteen now sir and I must see my family to safety," Wilfried said cautiously not wanting to anger the soldier. Wilfried knew full well of the shortage of men needed to fight back the Russians and feared that they would insist that he be enlisted on the spot.

Helmut watched, concerned as the officer just grunted and shoved the papers back into Wilfried's hands, while Auguste and Lydia sighed with relief. Wilfried climbed back onto the wagon and took the reins from his mother as he handed her the documents to stow safely. It was imperative that they had their documents available at all times.

"Mutti, keep these safe but handy. I'm sure this will not be the last time we will need them on this journey."

Wilfried then flicked the reins and their wagon moved forward slowly through the town, on the way to catch up with the wagons ahead of them.

Once they were through the city of Freistadt they were on their way to the Weichsel River, where they left the road to join the other wagons along the top of the levee or dam that ran along the bank of the river. For three days they followed the river, seldom stopping, since the levee was too narrow for wagons to pull over. The going was slow and sometimes the train was stopped due to unseen problems ahead. They would often find that a wagon had overturned into the river with its occupants aboard, or that an axel had broken and the refugees had no choice but to abandon it, releasing the exhausted, starving horses to fend for themselves.

One bitter cold evening they approached an abandoned wagon with a broken axel and found three little girls, younger than Helmut standing next to it, crying. Auguste pulled up the reins, stopping abruptly to speak with the children. "Where are your parents, Liebchen?"

The eldest of the three girls rubbed the tears from her eyes, looked up and shrugged. "They never came back."

Auguste and Lydia looked at each other distressed and Helmut cried, "Mutti, we have to help them!"

"But they could be separated from their parents forever if they go with us Helmut."

"But we can't leave them here to freeze," insisted Helmut, who looked at the other wagons that had passed them.

"Wilfried, help the girls onto the wagon. We will make room for them to sit on the back," instructed Auguste.

One by one, Wilfried lifted the children up to Helmut who helped his mother settle them under blankets at the back of the wagon on top of grain sacks for the horses. The girls seemed to relax, feeling safer and happy to be warm under the heavy horse blankets.

Helmut, content that they had not left the girls alone by the side of the road, snuggled into the blankets next to his sister to try to get some sleep as the wagon continued on in between two others in the train. It had been a few days since he'd slept and he was grateful to finally be able to close his eyes. It was late morning when he finally awoke to the hushed voices of his Mutti and Tante. The wagon train had fully come to a stop due to some delay ahead.

Helmut sat up and looked around for the three young girls they had picked up during the night. "Where are the girls Mutti?"

Lydia looked at Auguste and hesitantly answered, "We found their parents during the night and they took the girls, Helmut."

Helmut looked at them, confused, but happy with her answer as Wilfried flicked the reins for the horses to resume their journey. The wagon train continued on, passing abandoned town after town—all who lived there had vanished. It was as if the villages had turned to ghost towns overnight. For six days they traveled on their way to their first stop, which would be Preussich Stargard. There were empty buildings everywhere and the streets of every town lay desolate. On occasion, those from the wagon train would stop to check stores with open doors, to see if there was any food or supplies left behind. They passed people walking aimlessly—many desperate to find their loved ones. As they went, they scavenged anything they could find to eat that wasn't frozen, since edible food was extremely scarce.

Helmut walked much of the time, especially during the day, but the cobblestone roads through the towns were icy and slippery and he fell often. His shoes were too tight for warm socks so he walked to keep the blood circulating to his feet. During the dark nights the distant sounds of cannons and gunshot could be heard in the distance. It was like a dream from which he couldn't awaken and fear haunted Helmut. On occasion, a wagon or a passenger would be hit by stray bullets. They even encountered the German Army in hand-to-hand combat with the Russians a number of times. He wasn't certain if it was his imagination, but the guns sounded as if they were growing closer and closer. Perhaps it was just the silence of the frozen countryside, with only the light clomping of the horses' hooves and the squeaking of the wagon wheels as they rolled over the frozen earth.

•

For those family members and friends who had lagged behind—the ones caught by the Soviet Army—they were far unluckier than those suffering from cold, exhaustion, and hunger on the wagon train. Although many of Hitler's front-line commanders in Prussia requested permission to implement evacuation plans for women, children, and the elderly, Hitler felt the very idea smacked of defeatism and insisted that the province would be defended at any cost, rejecting all formal evacuation plans. The defense of the province was the responsibility of the Army Group Center, headed by General Georg-Hans Reinhardt, who oversaw the command of the Second Army, the Third Panzer Army, and the Fourth Army. So, no plan of any kind was ever drafted, even though the civilians had been promised protection from the Russians. It seemed, instead, they were totally on their own to fend for themselves. By then, rumors of the ruthless horrors of the Soviet Army had reached the citizens of Prussia and fear was welling by the minute in the minds of the fleeing multitudes.

Hitler's lofty aspirations to hold the province was a hopeless cause, since the German Army was massively outnumbered and the Soviets pressed forward with focused and unleashed ruthlessness, appearing as a mix of a modern and medieval army. There were Cossack cavalrymen on shaggy horses carrying stolen loot strapped to their saddles, tank troops wearing black helmets, horse-drawn carts pulling weapons, munitions and spoils, as well as common automobiles towing field guns. Since the German Army had little access to crude oil, it processed synthetic fuel from coal, but by the end of 1944, there was little fuel remaining for their Panzers and trucks, so much of their transport still relied on oxen and horses to pull their supplies and weapons. Much of the Red Army behaved barbarically—with many drunken soldiers armed with machine guns—there was little attempt by the officers to assert authority over their undisciplined men. Freebooters, drunks, and men so enraged by the desire for revenge against the injustices previously committed by the German Army, they had indeed become an army of murderers and rapists. Many Russian soldiers lined up to rape young women held spread-eagled on the ground—the men so hungry for sexual satisfaction and revenge they didn't discriminate the sharing of their prey, as their fellow soldiers gang-rapped their victims. In fact, they did not even discriminate concerning age, since women of ages ten to seventy were fair game. Women in hospitals, pregnant women, nuns, and mothers who had just given birth were victims of their brutality. Even Soviet women liberated along the way, were raped by their own countrymen.

Many women were viciously brutalized during the attacks and often died from their injuries. Most were raped in front of their children, husbands, mothers, other family members, and often in front of other citizens. Should any of their loved ones or voyeurs attempt to stop the attack they would instantly be killed. Their victims often begged for the soldiers to kill them, but instead of obliging, since they didn't believe in killing women and children, they simply stepped aside for their next comrade to have his turn.

Overall, a scorched-earth policy was implemented by the Soviets in general, as they shot wealthy civilians to steal their possessions, torched homes, businesses, and machinery, poisoned wells, and commandeered all food and resources, leaving civilians to starve, just as the Germans had done to the Russians.

CHAPTER 2

A Happy Childhood

1933 – 1944 — Ublick, East Prussia, Germany — Bischofswerder, West Prussia, Germany

As the distance grew from what he had known as home in the city, for the last five years, Helmut couldn't help but think back on his early childhood on the farm in Ublick, near the Polish border. He had only been five when Germany invaded Poland on September 1, 1939. By the time he was five and a half, the family had moved to the city of Bischofswerder, due to economic hardships from the war, but Helmut had always held fond memories of life on the farm. Although they had been poor farmers before moving to the city, his visions of that life still somehow brought back thoughts of happy times. Even if he had been a sickly child, suffering from pneumonia and scarlet fever. Often, Helmut had been left alone to fend for himself while his mother and father worked their modest farm, especially during harvest season. Luckily, he was a resourceful child and even at an early age managed to take care of himself, despite being timid if he was around other people. He always found activities to keep him occupied around the barn—playing in the hay, riding, Hans, the large but gentle, family dog, rounding up twigs for the fire to help his mother as well as gathering blueberries and wildflowers for the tea that his mother liked to make. Helmut fondly remembered picking wild mushrooms with his mother and the many fishing outings on the nearby lake with his father, when he was very young. Eventually however, he was making those fishing trips alone, due to his father's preoccupation with the farm. Their modest, but beautiful lakefront farm comprised of a small homestead attached to a barn which housed their animals, a hay and grain barn that housed food for their livestock: two horses to pull the wagon and the plow, four to five cows for milking, a few chickens for eggs, and anywhere from two to twenty pigs to feed the family and to butcher and sell. In between the house and the barn was a kitchen, where he remembered a huge kettle always boiling with some type of soup, usually made of pork, beets, cabbage, and potatoes. It was always Helmut's favorite job to give the leftovers, if there were any, to the pigs.

Helmut's life was quiet, but not lonely—always managing to occupy himself with something that kept him out of too much trouble. His father had made him a wooden sled so that in the winters he could slide across the frozen lake using two wooden stakes with nails to propel the sled across the ice.   Helmut thought fondly of his young neighbors, Gisla and Gertrhut, whom he played with often, even sharing his coveted sled with them. Some days Helmut would be given the task of watching one of the family cows that was staked on a chain in the pasture to eat the grass, or sometimes his parents would take him to the fields where they worked all day. There they would simply plop him on a pile of hay in the shade and let him entertain himself. But most of all he loved to go with his father to watch him whenever he was working with the horses. He always thought of the large beasts as oversized versions of his dog, Hans.

Helmut's fondest memories were of his grandfather, Johann Fester, who was born to German immigrant parents in Russia. He spoke four languages since as a young man; he had moved to Poland and had been drafted by the French Foreign Legion. He had been a preacher, but when the Germans invaded Russia, they made him a 'Political General,' rather than a professional soldier, due to his mastery of so many needed languages. His job had been to organize and supply food for the German Army and this often meant depriving the Russians of their much-needed food staples. Johann owned three farms directly on the border of Germany and Russia—so close in fact that the posts for the German defense lines, preventing vehicles from crossing the border, actually ran across his land.

Grandfather Johann was Helmut's favorite grandparent. Helmut had been born only one hundred kilometers from Johann's three farms and the family would often take the train to visit him, since there was a train-stop right in his grandfather's town. Helmut's mother, it seemed, was the apple of her father's eye—the youngest of three girls and two boys, which likely accounted for Johann's closeness to Helmut. Johann loved driving Helmut in his wagon around his farms, as well as the countryside. He even taught Helmut to play a game of cards, Schwatzkopf, using pennies to place bets. Of course, this greatly displeased Helmut's mother who was a very strict Christian of the Baptist faith. She took biblical doctrine very seriously, since as a young girl, she'd grown up with a father who was a preacher. She didn't believe in or approve of smoking, drinking, dancing, or gambling, but she found it hard to punish Helmut, especially when her own father was the one instilling the sin into the child.

•

Helmut's father, Gustav, had been drafted, the first time, by the German Army for training in the spring of 1934 and since the army didn't require troops during peacetime, he had returned to the family six weeks later, just before Helmut's birth on July fourth. Unfortunately, Gustav had suffered a leg injury during his basic training, from his boot-top causing an ulcer on his leg. The ulcer never totally healed and caused him constant pain and severely restricted his ability to work on the farm.

Events in Germany had taken a serious turn just before Helmut's birth when, Adolph Hitler, the leader of the Nazi Party, came to power on January 30, 1933, when President Paul von Hindenburg appointed him German Chancellor. Helmut Siewert was born seventeen months later, on July 4, 1934 and practically all of Helmut's early memories included Hitler as Chancellor of Germany and later as their Führer or Dictator. Upon Hindenburg's death, Hitler conveniently combined the position of Chancellor and President into the title, Führer. A national referendum on August 19, 1934, confirmed Hitler as sole Führer of all of Germany, forcing all German soldiers to swear to the 'Hitler Oath.'

•

World War II started on September 1, 1939, when Germany invaded Poland. The United Kingdom and France, in turn, declared war on Germany. Helmut had recently celebrated his fifth birthday and didn't understand the meaning of his country going to war, especially since the fighting was not directly visible to his young, yet curious eyes. However, he had even more curious and astute hearing and he absorbed all that he heard like a sponge. The closest Helmut came to direct contact with the war, during those years, was his father's obsession for listening to the war reports on the radio, especially Hitler's speeches. The radio reception was generally poor, but the fanaticism in Adolph Hitler's voice, as he talked of a new Germany and the glory of the Third Reich, was clear as day. Helmut knew that he must stay quiet, or his father would be angry should he miss part of the transmission. Helmut asked few questions of his father, but listened carefully to what the Führer said and he observed how his father responded to his speeches. Although he was too young to fully understand the meaning of this man's ranting and the cheering of the crowds, he tried his best to discern the meaning of what he said and how it would affect his family. Despite being young, Helmut doubted that much of what the Führer said was in fact the truth.

Although Germany was at war, life was peaceful in this bucolic, quiet part of East Prussia and although they were not personally touched directly by the war and the fighting, they were beginning to feel a shortage of food and supplies. This caused the family to move to the city of Bischofswerder in West Prussia, so that Helmut's father could take a well-paying job at the German Administration Office in the city. His job—oversee the German administration of the Polish people. It was a lucrative assignment with many governmental perks for the family, even if his father felt as if his work and the party ran contrary to his beliefs and his politics. He would eventually be forced to join the Nazi Party in 1944 in order to receive a promotion.

Overall, life was good, considering the chaos of the world around them. In those years, the war had spared the region of the fighting, death, and destruction that had been visited on the ground upon the major cities of Germany as well as from the British air raids. In 1941, America joined the war in the European Theater and the bombing raids doubled in the key cities of Germany, but spared most of the eastern part of the country. The planes simply couldn't fly that distance and return. The biggest impact that the war had on Helmut's homeland had been the drafting of most of the men sixteen to fifty-five years of age to serve, leaving the women and children home to fend for themselves. It wouldn't be long before Helmut's father would be one of them.

CHAPTER 3

Crossing the River — A Much Needed Rest

February 3, 1945 — The Weichsel River, Germany

When the wagon train finally arrived at the bridge to cross the Weichsel River, they saw that it had been destroyed by British and American bombings and there was no safe passage across. It was a fast-moving river, and as a result, the ice had not formed thick enough to make it viable for the wagons to pass. The German soldiers did their best to aid the refugees by spreading hay and water over the thin ice allowing it to freeze overnight. By morning, the zero temperatures had done their job by freezing the newly poured layer of wet hay into a thick ice bridge. When they tested the ice, they determined it to be solid enough to support the weight of the animals and wagons for crossing.

Quickly, the wagons lined up before the sun rose high enough in the sky to start melting the ice allowing a number of wagons crossed the river successfully. The wagon just ahead of Helmut's carried a family of four who had been traveling near them for the last few days. Time and the sun were their enemies now since the sun was getting high and the temperature was rising rapidly, creating a slushy surface over the top of the ice. As the wagon ahead started across, its rear wheels began to slide sideways on the ice toward the thin ice and the raging river. The older son, who was driving, cracked his whip at the horses to try and correct the slide, but the wagon was too heavy and the ice too slippery for the horses to pull it out of danger. As the rear wheel dropped off the thicker ice, it broke through, rolling the wagon over into the rushing river. The entire rig, with all family members aboard, was quickly pulled under by the strong current, including a young, blonde girl, who screamed for help as she fought her way to the surface as she was washed downstream. Then suddenly, there was a deafening silence as the forceful current sucked the little girl was sucked down for the last time. Everyone on the bank stood by helplessly watching as the entire family disappeared, swallowed up by the icy, raging Weichsel River.

Now it was Helmut's family's turn to cross and both Helmut and Wilfried slowly walked the horses across the ice bridge, tightly holding onto either side of their harnesses, careful not to excite them. As they cautiously crossed the ice, they all held their breath, praying their wagon would make it to the other shore. The ice was slippery and Helmut fell once, but luckily didn't spook the horses. It seemed to take forever to cross the short span of water, but once on the far bank of the river, they all thanked God for seeing them to safety. Helmut found it hard to talk to anyone about the tragedy he had witnessed on the river that day. The screams of that little girl—no older than he, haunted his dreams that night—her blonde hair swirling in the raging waters and her cries echoing in his head.

•

After traveling nonstop on the wagon for several weeks and passing through abandoned town after town, each of which lay desolate, the wagon train finally stopped for a break when they reached the city of Preussisch Stargard, east of the Oder River. In town, the German officials were still promising a turn-around in the war, with the hope of one of Hitler's 'wonder weapons/Wunderwaffe,' which was touted as the thing that would be their savior and stop the Russians in their tracks. The authorities truly seemed to believe the refugees would be able to return to their homes once this weapon arrived and they were told to stay put in Preussisch Stargard for the next few weeks. The thought of stopping to rest and prepare real, hot food was welcoming news to Helmut and his family and they once again held out cautious hope that maybe the promises of protection from the German authorities would come to fruition.

"Oh, thank God," exclaimed Auguste. "Maybe this weapon will be Germany's glorious salvation."

"I so hate to be the naysayer Auguste, but it would take a miracle from God to save Germany at this point," Lydia responded shaking her head.

Helmut, who walked with Wilfried guiding the horses through town, turned to his mother. "Mutti, what is a 'wonder weapon'?"

"I'm not quite sure Helmut, but it's rumored to be more powerful than anything we've ever seen."

It was arranged by one of the 'treck' leaders for many of the German refugees to sleep in a large barn with their fifty horses. Only a thin bed of hay was spread behind the animals and more than a hundred refugees slept together on the straw. It was far from comfortable, but the downtime allowed them to prepare food and thaw some of their frozen staples. Helmut and Wilfried selected a spot closest to the horses, since their bodies generated more warmth, and the boys lay nestled in the hay next to them. Due to their close proximity to the horses, they would occasionally receive something even warmer and wetter from the beasts. The latrines that were provided for the refugees were nothing more than a long, wooden log balanced over a trench. It provided little privacy and the women did their best to retain some semblance of modesty by covering themselves with their skirts. There was little water other than melted snow for cleaning oneself and the concept of a bath was a long-distant memory. All day long the German Army kept a large kettle of watery cabbage soup cooking for the refugees. In addition, they provided them with loaves of hard bread—one to each family. Most of the refugees had little food on their wagons and tried to barter rations from Helmut and Wilfried, since they had come so prepared.

The next day was sunny and the temperature had warmed somewhat, allowing Helmut and Wilfried to walk into town to assess the situation for better food and supplies. They'd been told that, in the mornings and evenings, organized meals were being arranged and distributed by the German Army for the refugees. When they arrived in the town square there was a crowd of people assembled watching something that seemed to be the center of attention. Squeezing through the crowd, the two boys slipped as close to the front as possible and found, to their shock and surprise, four men and one woman hanging dead from a gallows erected in the square. Each had a sign painted on their clothing which read, 'SPY.' If that wasn't shocking enough, in front of the gallows were eight bound and blindfolded men, who knelt in front of a row of German soldiers who had their rifles, trained on the prisoners. All of these men also wore signs, which read, "He who steals will be shot."

Suddenly, a German officer shouted, "Fire!" The ear-splitting crack of rifle-fire rang through the air, resounding loudly through the city streets as the eight men collapsed to the ground in pools of blood. Another group of prisoners were then forced at gunpoint to drag the corpses by the ropes that bound them, through the center of town for all to see. Helmut looked at his cousin with wide eyes and wondered if relieving the local, closed businesses of provisions was really worth getting shot.

"Maybe hunger looks better than the alternative, cousin," Helmut said still in shock.

"Yes….I don't think we'll be taking anything that we don't pay for in this town, Helmut."

Their reprieve in Stargard, during February, was a brief ten days before they could hear the distant sound of the Russian artillery closing in. Once again the eastern sky burned bright, with smoke filling the air. It seemed the Russians had managed to cross the treacherous river Weichsel and were being held off by the German soldiers as the Red Army ravaged everything in its path. Helmut and his family could see the German soldiers fighting the Russians in hand-to-hand combat with rifles, bayonets, and field guns, in an effort to protect the local farmers and refugees on the wagon train as they fled from the onslaught—the fighting pressing rapidly upon them.   Heinrich Himmler, Nazi military commander and the second most powerful man in the Third Reich, had given the order to launch one of the last German offensives against the approaching Soviets, called Operation Solstice.   The evacuation order was given to the refugees to flee the city at once and to head west, dashing any last hopes that the evacuees would someday return to their homes.

Quickly, Helmut and Wilfried readied the horses and the wagon. They ran alongside as Auguste drove, but once again it was pandemonium with all the other wagons trying to fall into line. As their progress through town slowed due to the other wagons, Helmut noticed men running from the open doorway of the town's butcher shop and thoughts of the men executed for stealing, in the town square, flashed through his mind. Although he feared retribution from the German soldiers, he realized that they were far too preoccupied to care if one little boy took a few sausages. The memory of fresh juicy sausage outweighed his fear and he made a quick decision, with the help of his rumbling belly, to leave the wagon and run into the empty shop. Once inside, he spied a dozen or so remaining sausages in the case and quickly grabbed two fistfuls of knockwurst, checked to see if anyone was watching, and ran back to the wagon train. He was quite proud of his prize however, the wagons had continued on in his brief absence and Helmut suddenly realized that Auguste had left him in the panic and chaos to flee the imminent arrival of the Russians as well as flying bullets. None of the wagons looked familiar and Helmut began to panic as he ran from wagon to wagon, through a sea of unfamiliar faces, looking for his family. He had heard stories of families losing their children in the mêlée and now he thought that he might turn out to be one of those unlucky children. He thought again about the three little girls who had been separated from their parents.

The chaos in the streets was creating total pandemonium as everyone pushed through town against the glut of horses, wagons, and humanity. After what felt like hours of searching, but in fact was only minutes, Helmut finally spotted his wagon. Exhausted, he was thrilled to see his Mutti and Tante, but his relief was short-lived as his panic-stricken mother scolded him sternly.

"I have been looking for you everywhere, where on earth did you go!" Lydia gasped in desperation, choking back tears. "We thought we had lost you in this madness! We were afraid that you may have ended up like those three little girls, crushed on the road at night!" Lydia caught herself, realizing she had done exactly the opposite of sparing Helmut and Marlene the harsh truth of their young passengers' demise.

"Oh Mutti, but you said they found their mother and father."

Stunned, Helmut nearly in tears, held up the sausages, "I'm sorry Mutti, I stopped to get these for us." The sight of his find in the butcher shop relieved some of Lydia and Auguste's anxiety.

"Just don't do it again! Do you hear me?"

"Yes, Mutti, I'm sorry," Helmut apologized realizing how foolish his rash decision had been, but imagining how delicious their dinner would taste if only they had a chance to cook the sausages. Helmut and Wilfried both climbed on the wagon since running alongside was far too dangerous. Then Helmut wrapped the sausages in paper and stowed them with the rest of their food. Suddenly, his mother's confession about the three little girls sunk in, "Mutti, I don't understand, how did the girls get crushed?"

"We didn't realize they jumped off the back of the wagon when you were sleeping," Lydia burst into tears. "They must have thought they saw their parents. When we realized they were gone, there was nothing we could do. Please Helmut, that's the last time we are going to discuss it." Lydia sniffled, wiping away her tears and trying to compose herself.

Helmut realized that asking more questions would be a mistake—it was one of those subjects the family just would never discuss. He felt extremely lucky that he had found his mother, considering the terror that was unfolding around them.

They passed a hospital, where sick and wounded soldiers who could walk were being evacuated, while those who were immobile were left with a dose of cyanide if needed. As the wagons drove out of town and into the countryside, many farmers were frantically harnessing up their rigs and piling belongings into their wagons. Others simply fled into the woods, on foot, with their families and whatever they could carry. The roads were clogged by the hundreds of refugees desperate to put distance between themselves and the Russian Army, which had started shooting at civilians from the air. The Russian aircraft had even begun dropping bombs in the inner city. Not only were the roads clogged with wagons, but the German forces pushing their way east cursed the civilians as they forced them from the road. "We will lose the war yet because of you! Get out of the way!"

CHAPTER 4

My Jewish Friend – Gone But Not Forgotten

1939 — Bischofswerder, West Prussia, Germany

That night, Helmut thought long and hard about his close call earlier in the day, when he thought he had been separated from his family. It was bad enough that he did not know where his father was, or if they would ever see him again, but the thought of being forever separated from his mother and sister was almost too much for such a young boy to comprehend. It made him think of a more peaceful time for the family, when they had first moved to the city in Bischofswerder and his father had taken his new job with the German Administration Office—overseeing the Polish people, since the Germans had taken control in Poland. They had run out of Nazi uniforms when Gustav went to work there, which made him happy since he didn't want to wear one anyway.

Gustav's boss was a Nazi who was far too overzealous about the Party. It didn't take long for Gustav to realize that he must play the part of a dedicated Nazi Party member, no matter if the abuse against the Poles and the Jews went against his own conscience. He had to look the other way when his boss would take his men to beat Polish farmers, forcing them to impart gifts, such as food and money, upon the administration.

Since the Administration building wasn't far from school, Helmut often visited his father at work after classes. It was there that he had his first taste and understanding of the ethnic differences between the full-blooded Germans, the Poles, and the Jews. This was a topic that was never discussed at home, although Helmut witnessed some of these differences when he met Polish people at his father's office. When he questioned Gustav about the things he'd observed there, his father was never forthcoming with any answers. The best he ever got out of him was, "This work I do is confidential and it is not to be discussed either at home or with others, do you understand, Helmut?"

"Yes, father but--"

"--as I said Helmut, it's not to be discussed, period. Now if you wish to continue visiting me at work you must agree to this, to not ask questions. Do you understand?"

"Yes, Father," Helmut would answer in frustration. So, he did as he had done all his life, trying to understand the role of the

Führer when he listened to the rallies and speeches on the radio—
he listened and observed.

It seemed that the Polish citizens were treated very differ-
ently than the German people. They were forced to wear the letter
'P' on their backs— known as the 'Ausweis,' or identification
card. Helmut learned just from witnessing some of his father's
interactions with the Poles who visited his office—those who
were Polish of German descent were slightly better off than those
who had no German blood at all. The Poles who had both blood-
lines were considered 'dual citizens' and not forced to wear the
letter 'P' on their backs. They were allowed to carry a German
passport however they were still considered second-class citizens.
They were provided more ration cards than the non-German
Poles and were allowed to join the German Army. Only a small
river separated Germany and Poland, but it may as well have
been an ocean. Even though it was his job to restrict the Poles'
freedom and lifestyle, Gustav tried his best to help these people
whenever possible without being obvious, but often he was required to even imprison them if the law demanded.

What Helmut hadn't quite figured out was why a few of
the people living in their village wore a yellow star on their
backs. He didn't yet comprehend what being Jewish meant and
how it would heavily determine the outcome of the war. The other thing he was unaware of at that time was that his father's

mother, Natalie Wagner, was, in fact, Jewish—a secret well hidden by the family. Also unknown to Helmut was that his father had forged documents stating that his mother was fully German with no Jewish blood to be found in the family lineage. Indeed, this family skeleton would make Helmut's blood one-quarter Jewish. His grandmother, Natalie, had been born in the Ukraine to a family with twelve children—six of who had died in the 1918 Spanish flu pandemic. She had married and grown to be a very strong woman, who ran her family farm with an iron fist. Helmut would often spend holidays on the farm working or playing with his cousin Wilfried—whose mother, Auguste, was Natalie's daughter. They lived on the adjoining farm and since Helmut was a bit afraid of his grandmother, who never hesitated to scold him if he did something wrong, he usually opted to stay at Wilfried's house rather than with his grandparents. Luckily, Natalie rarely resorted to corporal punishment with Helmut as she did with the Polish and French (both male and female) prisoners of the German Army who worked on the farm. But, even if she had, Helmut was confident he could easily outrun his very heavyset grandmother.

Witnessing his grandmother's cruel treatment of her workers made him realize just how serious the divide was between the workers and the German people, who had taken them captive after Hitler's invasion of Poland. Prior to the invasion

Hitler had given his army permission to kill, "….without pity or mercy, all men, women, and children of Polish descent or language." SS chief Heinrich Himmler added, "All Polish specialists will be exploited in our military-industrial complex. Later, all Poles will disappear from this world. It is imperative that the great German nation consider the elimination of all Polish people as its chief task." During the short Polish campaign, the German Army enacted no less than sixty-three actions against the Polish people. One commander maintained that, "Germans are the masters, and Poles are the slaves." And so it was that many Poles were taken as slaves and forced to work for the Army as well as the Administration. It was Gustav's job to find homes for many of these indentured prisoners, so he conveniently located a number of these slaves on his parents' farm.

Of course, Helmut was too young to fully understand that the women who worked in his grandparents' house, were, in fact, slaves and he grew to respect his grandmother's forcefulness against her 'workers.' Especially, when the punishment was corporal. The male slaves worked with his grandfather on the farm and Helmut noticed that he would be a little less cruel than his grandmother to the men working in the fields. Helmut would help his grandparents dig potatoes during his time off from school— usually three weeks in the summer, plus Christmas, Easter, and Ascension. He even enlisted some of his classmates from school to help and they would be brought to the farm via a truck that was powered by wood chips. Their job would be to clear the potatoes after the plow had passed, so they wouldn't be trodden by the horses when they plowed the adjoining row. In exchange, they would be given potatoes to take home to their families. By the time Helmut was nine, he was big enough to help his sickly grandfather, on the farm with the horses and the plow, a job that thrilled him since he loved any chance to work with the horses.

•

On his way to school everyday, Helmut would take a shortcut down a small street that was really no more than an alley. A year or so after moving to the city, Helmut started noticing a young boy, smaller than himself with dark curly hair, playing soccer alone in the alleyway. One day he stopped to talk to him, "Hi there, I'm Helmut, what's your name?"

The boy nervously looked around to see if anyone was watching them and shyly replied, "My name is Jacob."

"I've never seen you at school," Helmut said matter-of-factly. "Where do you study?"

"Well, I don't go to the German school, I study somewhere else." Jacob bounced the ball, "Do you want to play?"

"Sure, for a few minutes, but I can't be late to school." The two boys kicked the ball around the narrow alley lined with one-story homes with typical German roofs. Helmut suddenly stopped—his curiosity getting the better of him. "Where do you study?" Helmut persisted.

"Come back some afternoon and I'll show you. But….only if you can keep it a secret."

This of course piqued Helmut's inquisitive mind and he smiled and nodded, picking up his books. "I have to go now, but I'll be back, I promise."

Helmut walked through that alley every morning and afternoon on his way to and from school, but he didn't find his new friend, Jacob, playing soccer as he'd hoped. After a week had passed, Helmut went to the Administration Building to visit his father after school as planned that day. His curiosity had gotten the better of him and he had to ask a question of his father that he feared would not garner an answer. "Father, what does the yellow star on the back of people's clothing mean?"

Surprised, Gustav looked around and ushered Helmut into his office and closed the door. "It stands for Jew and it's something we do not talk about….especially here! All you need to know is that you are not to converse or play with them. Do you understand?"

"But....what is a Jew?"

"It's worse than being a Pole, so don't ask any more questions. Maybe it's best if you go on home today."

"Can we talk about it later?"

"Now I'm not going to say it again, Helmut. We don't talk about such things, just stay away from them!"

Disappointed and confused, Helmut walked home that afternoon through the little alley. Lo and behold, to his delight, there was Jacob kicking his soccer ball around the street, alone. Helmut stopped and dropped his books on the ground, smiling at his new friend who skillfully kicked the ball towards him. After a heated little volley between them a woman shouted from one of the porch stoops. "Jacob, I baked cookies. Bring your friend in and have some, dear."

Helmut looked at Jacob to make sure it was okay. Jacob nodded and smiled and they ran in for their afternoon snack. Jacob's house was a modest one-story with furnishings, not so different from his own home. It seemed Jacob's father was not around, but Helmut was afraid to ask about him in case he had passed away. Jacob's mother was happy that her son had a new friend and she treated Helmut kindly, asking many questions about his family. But, once he announced that his father worked for the German administration, as soon as Helmut, left she forbade Jacob see him again. It would be days before the two boys would meet up again in the alley and Jacob would uphold his promise to show Helmut why he was no longer in school. They made plans to meet on a Sunday afternoon at a burned-out old building that Helmut assumed was once a church. When Helmut arrived, he found his friend sitting on one of the remaining benches in front of the pulpit. Jacob's eyes lit up when he saw his friend and he stood to great him.

"What is this place and what happened to it?" Helmut inquired looking around at the missing ceiling and the huge stone masonry walls.

"It's a synagogue....it's where I went to school. I'm Jewish."

"That's why you have to wear that star on your back," Helmut surmised.

"Yes, it's the Star of David. Hitler does not like Jews and we are required to identify ourselves this way."

"You mean the way the Poles have to wear the 'P' on their backs?"

"Yes, something like that."

Helmut nodded, understanding now. "So, you went to school here?"

"I studied with the rabbi. To you he would be like a minister, or preacher, I guess."

"But what happened to it?" Helmut demanded. "How did it get like this?"

"The Germans did it. They don't want us worshiping so they took the rabbi away and burned the synagogue."

Helmut looked around with new understanding realizing now why his father insisted that he stay away from Jews. He thought about it and decided that a friend was a friend. It didn't matter to him that Jacob was considered an outcast by Hitler. He turned to Jacob and smiled, "Can we make this our meeting place?"

"Of course, it will be our secret!"

Helmut had heard stories of Kristallnacht —'Night of the Broken Glass'—when the Germans had destroyed Jewish businesses by looting and burning. It happened the year before Helmut had moved to the city, so he only knew of it second-hand. They had also destroyed the butchery, the grocery, a clothing store and many, many other small, family businesses that were Jewish-owned, even if they were establishments where Aryan Germans in their community shopped.

"So, this must have happened during Kristallnacht?"

Jacob looked down saddened by his question, "Yes, it was the Nazi Party's Sturmabteilung S.S. paramilitary forces. They called it the November pogrom."

•

Helmut thought that his newly acquired friend was a very bright boy who seemed to know of many more worldly things than Helmut, such as what a dictionary, an almanac, or an encyclopedia was and how to use them for learning. He also knew more about world history and geography, since he'd been schooled one-on-one by the rabbi. To Helmut, Germany was the whole world, and they were the conquerors, leaving him little desire to travel and leave the security of his homeland. But Jacob knew that there was so much more out there to be seen and learned and he did his best to broaden Helmut's diminished view of their world.

One night at the dinner table, Helmut grew brave enough to ask the forbidden question, "Why is it I can't be friends with a Jewish boy?"

His father stood up, "We already discussed that Helmut," and he walked to the living room and turned on the radio, closing the subject for good.

Helmut's mother insisted, "I hope you haven't been consorting with those people! It would be dangerous for your father….for all of us if you are seen with the wrong people. They are not equal to us, Helmut. Do you understand that?!"

"But this boy is very smart, smarter than me even!"

"I don't want to ever hear you speak of him again. And do not let me learn that you have seen him!" Lydia demanded.

With that Helmut gave up the discussion, realizing that his friendship with Jacob would have to be a furtive one. Although his parents disapproved, Helmut and Jacob secretly continued to be the best of friends for more than two years. He would lie to his mother and tell her that he had stayed after school to play with his classmates. The boys looked forward to their time together and the fact they had to meet covertly only added to their fun.

One day, when Helmut was eight, he arrived at the synagogue and Jacob was not there as planned. For several days he searched and even went to Jacob's home. What he found was a totally vacant house, stripped of all furnishings and personal items. It was almost as if Jacob and his mother had simply vanished, without a trace. He did however, find Jacob's soccer ball left in the alley where he last played. Helmut was devastated and confused at the loss of his closest friend. No matter how many times he asked his parents what had happened to the Jewish people—where had they disappeared to, the best he ever received as an answer to his burning question was, "We don't talk about it, Helmut. Never, ever mention it again….do you understand?"

Helmut was certain they knew where Jacob's people were going to, but he also knew that he would never receive answers to his questions from his parents. He'd heard rumors about prison camps, but until then his parents had shielded him with regard to concentration camps and the killing of Jews. He knew no other Jews, so for him there was really no one else to ask. He knew better than to ask at school for fear of causing his father problems, so he kept his many questions to himself.

CHAPTER 5

Trek to the Oder Neisse River – Train to Berlin

February 1945 — Preussisch Stargard, East Germany —
Neustrelitz, Germany

While the evacuees fled from the Russian Army as
it breached the city of Preussisch Stargard, west
of the river Weichsel, in Pommern, Germany, the
German Army pressed its way through the hoards, pushing the
terrified civilians from the road in order to get through. The Soviets had managed to make it across the river Weichsel with their
artillery and the sound of gunfire grew closer as Wilfried drove
the horses though the mêlée of wagons, soldiers, horses and
refugees, trying his best to avoid trampling anyone. Suddenly,
artillery shots exploded directly behind them as Helmut watched
in horror as two of the wagons were blown to bits, killing their
occupants. Splinters and body parts flew through the air all
around them and the chaotic sound of terrified screams and panic
washed over them as the mad rush to escape the Russians franti-

cally hastened. Wilfried cracked his reins again, screaming at the horses, driving them as quickly as they could go away from the gunfire, but the wagons ahead hampered their progress. Behind them in the city, Helmut could see Russian and German troops firing their weapons, and those who had run out of ammunition, engaged in hand-to-hand combat with bayonets. Russian planes flew low over them firing machine guns at the fleeing masses causing even more panic and hysteria. Young mothers desperately tried to protect their children, while older children shielded elderly parents, but they couldn't escape the frightening smell of gunpowder and death.

Along the outskirts of the city they saw Russian soldiers forcing residents from their homes at gunpoint and herding civilians into schools and churches as they ransacked and burned their houses. They shot out windows, dragged furnishings outside to use for firewood, and scavenged valuables and farm equipment for their own use. Worst of all, they heard the desperate screams of women being violated by Russian soldiers, in plain view, as their families watched.

•

Once the German Army passed the fleeing refugees their speed increased, but they could always hear the artillery behind them, creating constant pressure to keep moving forward as they made their way to the Oder River.

"What if the bridge is out over the river when we get there, Mutti?" Helmut asked his mother.

"It will be there Helmut, have faith. It will be there," she answered praying under her breath.

Helmut said no more, but also prayed she was right, since they would be trapped between freedom on the other side of the river, and certain annihilation if the Soviets had destroyed the bridge. Somehow his mother's confidence comforted him, although the family's anxiety heightened by the uncertainty and the knowledge that the Russians were right on their heels. Their Führer had deserted them with broken promises of protection and turning the tide of the war—Germany was not an invincible rock after all.

Helmut's worry of his father's whereabouts wore on him heavily and he hoped that his mother's confidence in Gustav's ability to find them would prove true. The family traveled non-stop the next thirty-some miles to the Oder Neisse River and as the days wore on, the family reached the point of near total exhaustion from the cold, the stress, their lack of sleep, as well as from the nerve-wracking sound of artillery behind them and planes overhead. Their horses, Hans and Liesel had been like machines—steadily pulling their wagon without complaint—but it now appeared that Hans had developed bleeding lungs from the stress and relentless pace. Since before Stargard he began to cough and sway as he walked, with droplets of blood appearing in his nostrils. All they were able to do for the poor creature was to hang a feedbag around his neck hoping to keep his energy up. When they finally reached the border at the river they were all relieved to find that the bridge was still intact, allowing them to cross it without difficulty.

As they pressed on into Germany, their wagon was stopped at three German checkpoints, to ensure that all evacuees fleeing west were not Jewish or full-blooded Poles. Each time the family held its breath and prayed as the soldiers examined their documents, hoping that they wouldn't study their papers too carefully since Auguste was born in the Ukraine and married in Germany. Their prayers were answered as each time they let Auguste pass without questioning the details of her birth.

After a few more weeks of travel, the weather grew steadily warmer and snowed less, allowing their food to thaw in the sun. They were relieved that they began to put distance between themselves and the Russians. Helmut walked on the road next to their wagon—with the warmth of the sun on his face and food in his belly, he began to hope that maybe life could be normal again. Eventually, they made it onto the Autobahn federal highway, where one lane was designated for refugee wagons and the remaining lanes for the military. The roads were no longer covered in snow and ice and their horse, Hans, had recovered from his bleeding lung.

They were covering around twenty kilometers a day and they even found food depots along the way that had been set up by the German Army. They no longer heard the guns, not because the fighting had stopped, but because the German Army had slowed the Russians' progress somewhat, allowing them to put more distance between themselves and disaster. This temporary calm afforded them the opportunity to stop at night, either sleeping in the wagon, or in farmers' barns bedded down with their livestock. By that point on the road, many families still remained in their homes, not feeling the pressing need to flee, since they firmly believed the German Army would be able to stop the Red Army from reaching them.

After three to four weeks of travel, the family's pace slowed and they entered towns where the German Army had set up food depots and services for the refugees. Wilfried and Helmut walked in the mornings and evenings to the government depots, where food was provided. Usually, they returned to the family with cabbage soup, which was cooked in very large pots—little else was available. At least the soup was hot and with the other stores from their wagon they were able to add protein to give them energy and keep their strength up. Sometimes the local farmers had enough to share with the refugees and their horses. The two families had also been given ration cards by the Army and there were towns where they could actually still purchase food in open stores.

Helmut and his family began to feel as if they had survived the worst of their ordeal and their mood was beginning to lighten. As they passed through the city of Stettin, late at night, the only sound they heard was the clicking of the horses' hooves on the cobblestone street. It almost felt as if they had left the war behind, to the east of them, since there were no Russian planes overhead, sounds of artillery or guns, or fires burning along the skyline. Stettin was eerily quiet and appeared untouched by the war, but as they passed through the center of town they came upon a gallows with the bodies of two men and a woman hanging with signs pinned to their clothes—'SPY.'

•

When they finally reached the town of Neustrelitz, East Germany, Lydia decided to leave the wagon, since Auguste was heading west to stay at her brother, Ewald's home in Visselhovede. Lydia's plan was to head south to stay with her cousin, August Fester, in the small town of, Schraplau southwest of Berlin, just outside the city of Halle. After their long and dangerous journey, however, Lydia decided her children needed rest before catching the train to Berlin. After inquiring with the townsfolk about lodging, they were able to find a woman in the town named Hilda, who lived alone in a two-story house. Not only was this kind woman willing to give them two rooms and a hot bath for several days, she refused to accept any payment from the family. It had been more than a month since the Siewerts had slept in a bed or had a hot bath—only the occasional opportunity to wash their hands and face in icy cold water. It was the first bath that Helmut would have since they left their home back in Bischofswerder and he thought it was by far the best bath he'd ever had. It also afforded them the opportunity, with the help of a little kerosene and a bar of soap, to kill the lice in their hair and wash their filthy clothes. Unfortunately, the lice were quite resistant to the kerosene and Helmut found it necessary to shave his head to rid himself of the parasites. Although parasite-free, he looked rather pitiful with his totally baldhead full of sores from all the scratching. Marlene took one look at him and broke out laughing.

"Mutti, look at me, I look ridiculous," lamented Helmut.

"Helmut my dear, at least you're alive to have a bald head. And it appears it's the first thing to make your sister happy since we left."

With that, Helmut started making funny faces for Marlene, who laughed so hard her sides started to hurt. "That's okay, enjoy yourself at my expense! You're just lucky we didn't have to shave your head. You didn't sleep in the straw with the horses."

Once they had cleaned up, their host prepared them a wonderful dinner that night, with savory meat and fresh vegetables—Helmut thought that it was perhaps the best food he could ever remember. Never before had such a simple meal tasted so good. That night, when he went to sleep on the horsehair mattress with his mother and sister, it felt like heaven and Helmut slept like a baby for the first time in weeks. He dreamed he was back on the farm with his dog, Hans, playing in the hay in the summer sun, instead of running from soldiers and bombing raids.

The second morning in Neustrelitz Hilda helped Lydia work out the train schedules to Berlin. Lydia hadn't traveled much and was inexperienced with such things. She purchased three train tickets from Neustrelitz to Berlin, where she was told she would have to switch to the underground subway in order to catch the train to Schraplau. The morning after their second night, the Siewerts' parting with Auguste, Wilfried, and Pauline was emotional and difficult for the two families. Helmut had grown incredibly close to his cousin over the last six weeks, even more so than ever before. There was nothing like a war to make you realize how important family is in your life. Although they had always been friends who played together, their age difference had put them on unequal terms—Wilfried being four years older and in a different school. Also, the few kilometers distance between their homes since Wilfried lived in Konradswalde, down the road from Helmut meant that they only saw each other on special occasions, holidays and summers on their grandparents' farm. But the trials they had just survived together had created an incredible bond between them and put them on an equal footing. Helmut had matured years in only a few weeks and Wilfried respected his young cousin's strength and bravery. Both boys felt as if they'd somehow graduated from childhood into manhood after their long, arduous journey. Helmut knew he would miss Wilfried terribly. He had no friends where they were going, but his mother assured him that he would make new ones quickly once they reached their new home.

Auguste, Wilfried, and Pauline continued on in their wagon, traveling west to Ewald's home in the small town of Visselhovede. He had recently been drafted into the German Army and Auguste planned to stay there with Ewald's wife, Elfriede, who now occupied their home alone. Lydia, Helmut, and Marlene boarded the train to Berlin and Halle, with a plan to transfer to the small city of Schraplau, where August, Lydia's cousin on her father's side, lived with his wife Mary. Helmut wasn't sure how his mother knew, but Lydia been given information that the

Americans would likely reach Schraplau before the Russians and she felt they would be in safer hands with the American Army. Lydia was a little worried as their arrival would be unannounced, but she hoped that Mary would welcome them as family and allow them to stay until they could find a place of their own.

The next morning as they sat at the Neustrelitz station waiting for the train to Berlin, Lydia wondered if she had done the right thing—would the train really come this time? If she'd only known the truth about her missing family members, fretting over the train would have seemed minor. She had no way of knowing that Auguste's husband, Johann, had been captured by the Russian Army and was imprisoned in Prussia and her own husband, Gustav, had been taken prisoner by the Americans and was being held in central Germany. She also did not know that Gustav's brother, Herbert, had been separated from his wife, Olga, who had lagged behind and was captured and raped by the Russians. Not to mention that Lydia's brother, August, had also been separated from his wife, Elke, and twelve-year old daughter, Ingrid, who were captured by the Russians and turned into sex slaves.

On April 30, 1945, less than sixty days after Auguste and Lydia departed Neustrelitz with their children, the Red Army troops of the 2nd Belorussian Front entered the town, resulting in the suicides of more than six hundred residents.

CHAPTER 6

Hitler's Youth – Jungvolk

July 4, 1944 — Bischofswerder, West Prussia, Germany

As they sat at the station, waiting for the train in Neustrelitz, having barely escaped with their lives from the invading Russian Army, Helmut thought back on his friend Jacob. On the way to the station he had seen many signs reading, "No Jews Allowed." There had been many rumors around their encampment in Stargard and around the town of Neustrelitz about where all the Jews had been taken. He prayed the rumors were false since he couldn't imagine his best friend being subjugated to the horrors he'd overheard about the concentration camps in Prussia, where Jacob and his mother had most likely been sent. It was said that young, strong teenage boys who were capable of manual labor were spared the gas chambers and put to work. However, those considered children, along with their mothers, were put to death upon arrival in the camps. Helmut knew that Jacob had been smaller than him in stature at eight, even though he felt his friend to be older than him in knowledge. He couldn't bear the thought of such a smart, compassionate boy becoming one more casualty of this horrible war. He remembered how lonely he'd been after Jacob's disappearance. It had left a huge void in his life—not one of his other friends matched Jacob's understanding and worldly intelligence. Jacob had indeed been one of his most important teachers and had broadened Helmut's desire to explore the world. He also inspired him to start reading books with a voracious appetite.

Not long after Jacob disappeared, the German Administration had forced the local citizens of Bischofswerder to take in child evacuees from surrounding cities farther to the west, who were forced to flee the American and Allied bombing raids. Hans, a young boy around Helmut's age, had come to live with them. He, and many other children were evacuated from the city of Aachen, for fear they'd be killed in the bombing raids. They had been sent to Bischofswerder, since it was far enough to the east that the bombers leaving on missions from England couldn't reach them to drop their load of bombs.

Hans was a nice, but shy boy and Helmut tried to make friends with him. However, compared to Jacob, he was disappointed that Hans was not as bright, interesting, or exciting. Helmut felt as if he always had to carry their conversations and help him fit in at school, if that was even possible since he was so awkward. Helmut himself bordered on shy, so in some ways it helped pull Helmut out of his shell. Even though Helmut knew they would never become best friends, he still went out of his way to make Hans feel at home in their modest little three-story walk up.

Hans and Helmut were in the same grade as Helmut, so they walked to school together everyday and Helmut did his best to introduce the boy to his fellow classmates and friends. The boys would usually play soccer after class, as well as engage in a plethora of shenanigans that boys get into, such as climbing onto the roof of the sports hall to see who was brave enough to jump off. There was always a mandatory two hours of homework, so their playtime was limited to a coveted hour, once their five hours of classes had let out. Hans tried his best to fit in, however, he always seemed a bit of an awkward outcast to Helmut.

Of course, Bischofswerder still hadn't seen the advent of indoor plumbing, so Hans was not used to the concept of a pot under the bed, or getting up in the middle of the night to go out into the cold to relieve himself in the outhouse. From the time he arrived at the Siewert home, he struggled with bedwetting, which greatly distressed Lydia. Washing bedclothes without plumbing was a very laborious chore and she had to wash Han's sheets so often it quickly became a terrible strain on her. Lydia felt sorry for the boy and did her best to tolerate the terrible inconvenience, hoping Hans' bad habit would improve, but after nearly two years of doing extra laundry, she contacted Hans' mother and requested to send him home. His mother granted her wish and Lydia immediately purchased a train ticket for Hans to return to Aachen. Although Helmut felt bad for the boy and worried for his safety, he was secretly relieved that Hans was gone.

•

On their daily walk home from school, the boys passed the home of a younger boy named, Erich, who suffered from hydrocephalus, a condition caused by the build-up of fluid in the brain. The other boys would call him cruel names like water-head and balloon-head, but Helmut felt sorry for Erich and scolded them each time they shouted mean taunts at him. Aside from his disfigured head, the boy was unable to attend school due to his many symptoms from the disease, such as headaches and dizziness. His unsteady gate and his tendency to fall due to his weakened legs made the boys tease him that much more. He would sit on the porch stoop everyday watching the other children walk to and from school, even though he knew they would torment him, but Helmut could see that Erich was so lonely for some sort of friendship that the taunts didn't even matter. Even the torment seemed to be better to him than the loneliness.

On days when Helmut didn't have a lot of homework, he would stop and talk with Erich, who he found to be quite intelligent even though he'd never been to school. After many months of begging his friends to stop picking on the poor boy, their non-compliance and lack of compassion for the child's condition finally tore a rift in Helmut's friendship with a few of his classmates. He did, however, manage to remain friends with one of his classmates, Manfred. He and Manfred would go a local butcher shop, owned by Manfred's aunt and uncle in the afternoons to help out in return for food for his family This effort was greatly appreciated, since all citizens were on strict food ration cards and it seemed there was never enough food for the family. Once in a while, Manfred would invite Helmut to drop by the shop on Saturdays so he could sneak him a few ring bologna hotdogs—something his father loved.

Helmut always suffered from a strained relationship with his father, who never really made Helmut feel loved. In fact, he had heard stories that Gustav actually had suspicions that Helmut was not his own progeny. It seemed that the timing of his conception had been close to the time when his father was first drafted into the Army for basic training. Helmut had arrived earlier than the expected due date so the timing of his birth had fallen into a somewhat questionable category. It seemed that the local Baptist minister made it a habit to stop by to check on Lydia during Gustav's absence, making her husband suspect Helmut's actual genetic makeup. It was the new shoes that the minister had given Lydia that ignited Gustav's suspicions. He couldn't understand why a man, not her husband, would care about her footwear. So, due to Helmut's ongoing desire to please his father he asked a favor of his friend Manfred—help him acquire his father's favorite dish—ring bologna sausage. Even without the required ration cards, or any form of payment, Manfred was able to sneak Helmut three of the most amazing, large sausages as a gift for his father. When Helmut arrived home that day and presented the sausages to Gustav, it was the first time he remembered receiving his father's show of appreciation and love.

"My friend Manfred gave me these sausages for you today, Papa."

Gustav's eyes grew wide when he saw the sausages and he received them with his stomach already starting rumble in expectation. "Oh my, are you sure you didn't steal these Helmut?"

"Of course not, Papa. I help out at the store sometimes in the afternoons in exchange for food."

"Well, then any day you want to take off from work around here, by all means go ahead help your friend. And, tell him thank you. But do you think they might have some knockwurst next time?"

"I'll see what I can do to get them for you," offered Helmut realizing he'd found Gustav's weak spot—his stomach.

Gustav hugged Helmut for the first time that he remembered and walked away happy with Helmut's gift. Had Helmut realized that all it would take to win his father's love were a few measly hotdogs, he would have made it his job to get them long ago.

•

In the summer of 1944, just before Helmut's tenth birthday, Lydia got word from her mother that her father had been butchering a pig on his farm and simply dropped dead of a heart attack. Lydia was beside herself and Helmut was very sad since Johann was his favorite grandparent. Lydia and Helmut took the train from Bischofswerder to his grandfather's farm for the funeral. When they arrived, they found that there was a shortage of bedrooms in the house, due to the fact that other family members had unexpectedly come to attend the funeral. It was so crowded in fact, that Helmut ended up sleeping in his cousin Edeltraut's bed. He thought she was a very pretty girl, but she was four-years his elder and he felt a bit intimidated by her age and her beauty. Helmut had offered to sleep on the floor, but Edeltraut managed to coax him into the bed next to her, insisting that there was plenty of room for both of them. That's when Helmut learned that she had evidently been schooled in more than just scholastics. During the two short nights that Helmut spent in her bed, she taught him many things. Her instruction started with hugging and kissing and by the time Helmut had matriculated from Edeltraut's school of lovemaking his innocence was lost. After two days, Lydia noticed the attraction between them and decided to move Helmut to another room. It seemed however, that Helmut and Edeltraut had already become true, kissing cousins. It was a very young age for Helmut to learn about girls, but then he was already quite advanced for his age in many things.

•

The war carried on and it was quickly approaching Helmut's tenth birthday on July the fourth, which meant he would be expected to join the ten to fourteen year-old division of the Hitler Youth group—Young Folk, or Deutsches Jungvolk. Because his father worked for the Administration, Helmut knew he would be unable to decline the invitation to join with his friends and classmates. To most, it was a great honor to become part of the Nazi Party at such a young age, but other than the thought of being able to do organized sport such as soccer, gymnastics, running, rope pulls, hurdles, and other events, Helmut wasn't thrilled with the idea. He especially hated learning to march in unison—a requirement before they were allowed to play sports. The family knew that the children who refused to join the youth organization in the past had been taunted by their peers and some students were even denied their diplomas. Refusing to join could very well keep them from any chance of entering the university, or taking an apprenticeship, making membership in the organization quite mandatory.

Both girls and boys were organized into their own local 'cells' and Helmut was to soon be inducted into his community cell. He liked the thought of the camping, fishing, and hiking outings, as well as the camaraderie, however the indoctrination of the Nazi ideology went against the grain of Helmut's conscience. He especially rejected their belief that only pureblooded Germans were good enough to join. Their enemies were Jews and Poles and they were taught to hate them and treat them as outcasts to society. It made Helmut think of his friend, Jacob, and it saddened him that he had disappeared, affording him the sudden realization that even if Jacob was still around, it would have been impossible for them to associate.

Jungvolk's new recruits were designated 'Pimpfen,' which meant Upper German. A group of ten boys were known as Jungenschaft, with the older boys as their leaders—four of these groups were called a Jungzug. The magazine called, 'Der Pimpf' was aimed at brainwashing the young boys by enticing them with outrageous propaganda and promises of great adventure. Their uniforms were black shorts and a tan shirt with pockets, a rolled black neckerchief and topped off with a tan side cap. The color of the cap's piping designated what unit each boy was in. Their emblem was a white Sieg rune on black—a symbol of victory— worn on a patch on their upper left sleeve. They were never allowed to carry anything in their pockets other than a comb and a clean handkerchief. The uniform made Helmut feel somewhat foolish, but he had no choice but to comply. On a summer day in June, 1944 the induction ceremony was held in a large, modern gymnasium with parquet flooring, chairs for the boys to sit on, and a stage in front. After listening to the leader of their Jungenschaft wax on about the attributes of the Nazi Party and how honored they should feel to become a member of the Jungvolk, the boys were sworn in. With his hand in the air, Helmut repeated the oath, "In the presence of this blood banner which represents our Führer, I swear to devote all my energies and my strength to the savior of our country, Adolf Hitler. I am willing and ready to give up my life for him, so help me God." And with those words, Helmut and the other boys were officially inducted into the organization.

At the end of the swearing-in ceremony, they were to walk to the front to individually be acknowledged by the leader, as well as some of the older boys from Hitler Youth. Helmut, being near the front of the auditorium, was one of the first boys to approach the stage. He assumed that the appropriate thing to do was to shake the leader's hand, since his mother and father had always instilled these customary manners in him. When he nervously arrived on stage he offered his hand to the leader in the gesture of a handshake, but the man just stood there and promptly raised his right arm shouting, "Heil Hitler," the Nazi or Sieg Heil salute. The other boys snickered and chuckled at Helmut's massive faux pas, embarrassing him as he quickly corrected his greeting, mimicking the leader in the brown Nazi Party uniform with a swastika armband, as opposed to the grey uniform of the German Army.

As he slunk away from the stage in humiliation he realized he should have known what protocol to follow, since it was expected of every child to give a Hitler salute to pretty much everyone they met throughout the day. Now that he was officially a Hitler Youth, it was a must—otherwise such an offense could be punishable by law.

Once inducted into the Young Folk, one of the boys' jobs was to collect materials capable of being recycled—paper and scrap metal, being their group's primary focus. They were also required to act as messengers in the civil defense organizations—Reichsluftschutzbund (RLB). For this job as messengers the boys were trained in firefighting, protection against chemical weapons, and preparations of houses and apartments for air raids. While training in the area of sport, Helmut played soccer, practiced rope climbing, running, vaulting, and other gymnastics as well as mandatory calisthenics, pull-ups, and sit-ups. Camping in tents became an important summer activity, allowing the boys to learn outdoor skills, something Helmut really enjoyed. He was also looked forward to the future prospect of high jumping as he watched the older boys train. Some of the boys in his 'cell' had running shoes, Helmut included thanks to his father, but there were a few that had to run, march, and train in bare feet.

The girls, or League of German Girls or Maidens, (Bund Deutscher Mädel, or BDM), were trained separately. Sometimes however, they would be on the same field giving the boys a chance to watch their colorful routines and gymnastics with banners and flags—all performed to music. They also played a type of soccer using their hands to dribble the ball down the field to what looked like soccer goals, as well as Korfball, a sport akin to basketball, played on an indoor court. Unlike the boys, the girls remained members of the Hitler Youth until they turned twenty-one years old.

The Nazi Party always encouraged the girls to be promiscuous hoping to encourage the propagation of the German Aryan race. They even implemented a welfare state, where girls and woman received a Kidergeld supplement of money for every child over three babies to which they gave birth to. The important thing for the girls was to be beautiful and healthful. Their main goals in life were to follow the church, be good in the kitchen to please their men, and of course first and foremost, bear children for the Führer. For the Hitler Youth magazine and print-ed propaganda, the Nazi party selected the most beautiful of the girls and the most handsome statuesque boys to represent their perfect Aryan image, promoting the idea that all good things came from Hitler Youth. Likewise, the SS German police, and the military chose only the most perfect male and female specimens to represent the Arian race in their propaganda.

•

As time went on, Helmut felt his Young Folk meetings were akin to military exercises and training and the doctrine felt dominated by Hitler's totalitarian dictatorship and National So-cialism. Both the girls and boys were taught to die for their coun-try and their Führer. The Nazi flag meant more than life itself and in public it was a requirement to raise an arm when ever in its presence. These children, both boys and girls, were the hope of Germany's future. They were required to attend all local Nazi Party rallies and parades and every Wednesday there was a meet-ing for the sole purpose of pure indoctrination, which Helmut at-tended. There was little joking or frivolity, just a heavy air of se-rious focus. The only good Helmut saw in their coming together was the lack of social distinction—poor kids rubbed shoulders with the rich and differing backgrounds did not affect how they were treated—they were all equals.

Helmut especially disliked how they encouraged the children to inform on their own parents, to the authorities, if their family's beliefs were in opposition to the Nazi agenda. He actually knew members who had reported family members to the SS for actions they deemed to be disloyal to the Party. Only two months after he'd been inducted, his leader, Juergen, who was barely fifteen himself and in charge of one hundred fifty boys, approached Helmut giving him a salute, which Helmut returned.

"Helmut, it has come to my attention that you excel in most every activity and I intend to promote you to the next rank by early January. This means you will be awarded your knife."

Helmut knew that the knife was an important symbol of achievement for the boys and he was a little caught off guard by the young man's praise.   "Well….thank you Juergen….but why me? There are many boys here that deserve this more."

"I have high hopes for you in 1945, Helmut. You show great promise for the Nazi Party. You simply must push yourself to be more outgoing and confident. Also, I would like to see you being more active in the organization."

"Well thank you, I will do my best," Helmut answered, but what he really felt was that he would like to have less interaction with the Nazi Party.

By this point, Helmut had already attended one of the huge outings at a large field stadium, where they all performed gymnastics and a routine. He and fourteen other boys in his 'cell' were driven to the location in the nearby city of Deutsch-Eylau in West Prussia, in an open dump truck. It was all very exciting, with hundreds of other boys and girls at the event performing and chanting Nazi rhetoric, however, he felt torn between his feelings about the ideology versus being a part of something so seemingly important to his country. At these events the children competed in National sports competitions where certificates and badges were awarded for proficiency. The children were expected to be swift as greyhounds, tough as leather, and hard as steel.

When Helmut saw the older boys training and competing in the use of small rifles, obstacle courses, complete field exercises that included military-like training with hand grenades, courage tests, war games, and heavy terrain maneuvers he started to worry that he would also be groomed for the military. Becoming a soldier was the last thing Helmut wanted for his future. He hoped and prayed that the war would be over soon, but it seemed to just stretch on and on. Rumors spread that the Russians were gaining territory towards the eastern front and it seemed as if

Germany's only future was an ongoing war without an end in sight. The frightening part was that it seemed to be growing closer and closer to their doorstep. The German Army was so desperate it was starting to force boys younger than sixteen to serve as aides to soldiers actively fighting in battle, even though they were too young to be officially drafted as soldiers. The older boys and girls were often placed in the jobs left vacant by those old enough to be drafted—jobs such as working on farms where crops were grown for the military.

Helmut knew that when he reached his fourteenth birthday, he would graduate to the Hitler Youth and would be at risk of being forced onto the battlefield to assist German soldiers as aides. At sixteen he would be drafted and then at the age of eighteen, he would be forced to join the Party. The Nazi Party controlled the schools as well as all competition through Hitler's Youth and although he was too young to read Hitler's manifesto, "Mein Kampf," it was drilled into him and his fellow classmates in Hitler School, that God and Hitler looked out for them and the future of Germany. Due to the shortage of educators, one of his teachers was, in fact, his cousin, Edeltraut, who had only attended school for a few years herself. This surprised Helmut since he already knew far more about academics than she did; yet she was assigned to teach him and his classmates. It was also quite awkward that she had been the one to instruct him in a more personal field of education on that trip to his grandfather's funeral. Edeltraut knew how smart Helmut was so she often requested his assistance in tutoring the other children in his class, making it seem as if he were a somewhat privileged recipient of nepotism. The school's facilities and scholastics were drastically lacking and a number of ages were taught together, but at least the school did provide the boys and girls with private, separate toilets inside the schoolhouse, with pots or buckets under the toilet seats, as opposed to outhouses in the dead of winter.

By September of that year, Gustav had been called back to the army and forced to join the Nazi Party, even though he still had the serious leg injury and found it difficult to walk long distances. By this point in the war, the Nazis were desperate for any men, able or not, to fight against the fast approaching Russian Army.

Helmut's activities with Young Folk continued, including another outing to the town of Deutsch-Eylau. The huge stadium held over twenty thousand girls and boys and the seats were filled with an adult audience. It was all very exciting as Helmut watched the older boys do their military drills and the girls their colorful dance routines, rousing an extreme patriotic fervor amongst the crowd. Helmut's 'cell' had developed a successful soccer team and they were quite successful at beating the opposing 'cells' in many matches, making Helmut and his teammates local heroes.

However, at the start of the new year, before Helmut's leader, Juergen, had had a chance to promote him, Helmut found himself fleeing for his life with the Russian Army on his heels.

CHAPTER 7

<u>The Bombing – Buried Alive</u>

Early March 1945 — Berlin, East Germany

Lydia, Helmut, and Marlene sat waiting for the train at the station in Neustrelitz, Germany, to take them to Berlin. Lydia worried whether the train would actually arrive, after what they'd experienced on the first morning they had fled. When she finally heard the whistle blow from around the bend she breathed a huge sigh of relief.

"Oh thank God, we are going to be fine now children, the train has come."

It wasn't until that moment that Helmut realized his mother had her doubts about their safety. He smiled at her and squeezed her hand and she smiled back. Her young son had grown up quickly under the unimaginable strain of the past several weeks.

It took a while for refugees to disembark onto the platform and for them to call for passengers to Berlin to board however, the passengers lined up the minute the mass of people had cleared the platform. Through the pushing and shoving, Helmut struggled with the cases as his mother carried Marlene, who looked at the train in amazement. Helmut was excited as they boarded the train for the half-day trip to Berlin. It reminded him of happier times and the train trips he took with the family to visit his grandparents.

Once aboard, they realized how primitive the train was with its wooden benches instead of seats, but the Siewerts were so relieved to be on it, they would have been happy to stand, or to sit on the floor. The train made good progress on its way to Berlin, with only a few small town stops and a couple of pauses to clear the tracks of rubble from the Allied air raids. They had heard a few reports about the destruction in Berlin, but as they neared the city, it was hard to believe the devastation left from the bombings by the Allied Forces on February third and the twenty-sixth. Many buildings in the city had been leveled and people wandered around, digging in the rubble for their loved ones and any possessions they might find. The military was attempting to clear the streets of the rubble, but it was an overwhelming task. Because most of the troops were needed elsewhere, there were many civilians aiding the soldiers. There were still a few buildings standing, but every one of them showed signs of distress from the bombings. Lydia tried to distract Marlene from being scared by the sight, but Helmut took it all in trying to understand how one nation could do such a thing to another.

"Mutti…." he implored, "Will life ever be the same again, or will we have to run forever?"

Lydia put her arm around Helmut. He was a man now and it was important for her to be honest. "Helmut, I wish I could say it will all be okay, but there is so much hatred in this world. Let's pray the Americans will save us. You know we have family in America," Lydia said hopefully. "Your Aunt Helen lives there in a state called Wisconsin. Maybe we will go there someday."

Helmut sat speechless, watching as the train slowly rolled into the Berlin station, shocked that his mother could actually think it could be the Americans, not Adolph Hitler, that would make things right again.

•

Unbeknownst to the Siewerts, Hitler was, at that moment, hiding out from the carnage, in that very city in his underground Führerbunker with his mistress, Eva Braun. The bunker was very close to the Reich Chancellery and the Gestapo headquarters' main security office on Prinz-Albrecht-Strasse. The Führer's residence below ground was in the lower, newer section of the bunker and consisted of Hitler's private guest room, his sitting room, his study/office, and Eva's bedroom. There was also a waiting room outside of the conference room with a large map and a painting on the wall of his hero, Frederick the Great, who had been the King of Prussia from 1740 until 1786. He was the last monarch to be titled king and had been a major military power in Europe during his rule.

All of the furnishings and art in the Führerbunker had been stripped from the Chancellery to make Hitler feel more at home. A generator provided electricity, fresh water was pumped from a well, and pumps to the surface removed excess groundwater. There were sufficient food stores to last for years, and every source of communications had been installed, such as telex, telephone, switchboard, radio, as well as an army radio with and outdoor antenna were installed. In the level above Hitler were administrative offices for staff members such as secretaries, medical personnel, and a switchboard operator. Other administration staff members were also housed there, along with Joseph Goebbels and his wife and children. Hitler received outside news from the BBC radio as well as via courier.

•

When Helmut, his mother, and sister got off the train, Lydia asked for directions to the underground subway that would take them through Berlin to another train, which would connect to the city of Halle, where they would then transfer to Schraplau, their final destination. When they arrived at the subway station there were hordes of people pushing and shoving to get on the train. Helmut and Lydia found it necessary to also push their way through to the front of the line. As the doors opened and the crowd ahead of them forced its way on, Helmut stepped aboard and turned to see his mother and sister pushed aside by several men determined to board before the doors closed. They pushed Helmut back and the doors closed before Lydia and Marlene could make their way on. Marlene was crying and Lydia panicked, screaming for someone to help, as she watched her son taken away by the swiftly moving subway train. Helmut screamed, "Mutti!" and banged on the door trying to force it open, but to no avail, he was trapped and flying away from his mother faster than he could think.

Lydia ran to the platform attendant asking if they could bring the train back to the station and the man just laughed at her. "Frau….that train is gone. Wait for the next one and try getting off at the next station. If your boy is smart he will get off at the next stop just down the way." With that advice, the man just turned and walked away leaving Lydia standing there holding her screaming daughter in her arms.

"Mutti, where have they taken Helmut?"

Squeezing her daughter to assure her, Lydia said unconvincingly, "He's meeting us at the next station."

Helmut panicked for a few moments and then realized that there would be another stop two to three kilometers ahead, as he'd learned when he'd studied the board that mapped out the underground train's route. When the train stopped at the next station, he stepped off first and stayed as close to the door as possible to wait for the next train to come. As the train pulled away, he asked the passing attendant, "Herr, how long will it be before the next train from Berlin comes?"

"Should be one hour on the dot unless we have some delay on the tracks."

"Thank you," replied Helmut somewhat relieved, but nervous that his mother would instead wait at the other station for him to return. As promised, an hour later the train pulled into the stop and the doors slid open. There, in front was his mother, whose face beamed with relief when she saw him. She ran and grabbed him, hugging him and kissing the top of his head.

"You're such a smart boy! How did I ever raise such a smart lad? Were you scared?"

"No not really, I knew you'd find me Mutti." Helmut lied trying to hide his relief.

Lydia was worried that they might miss the train to Halle, so they quickly pushed their way back onto the crowded subway and did their best to find a place to sit. Lydia sat with Marlene in her lap and Helmut stood hanging onto the post. The subway train took off from the station underground and traveled only a few minutes, when suddenly they heard a frightening rumbling sound, which rocked the train. The train shuddered to a stop and there were several terrible explosions that nearly knocked the train off the track as dirt and concrete rained down from above. Helmut fell to the floor and grabbed his mother's leg as she shielded Marlene. Passengers screamed, the lights flickered on and off and then suddenly all went dark on the train, and in the tunnel. A number of passengers screamed, "Bomb!" while others cried in terror. All was suddenly quiet, except for the sound of dirt falling on the roof of the train. No announcement came from the conductor and the passengers could only guess for themselves what had happened. The regular, experienced riders knew there had been more bombings above ground and supposition quickly spread through the train cars. One hysterical passenger screamed, "We're buried alive!"

Marlene started to cry as Lydia hugged her tightly and rocked her trying to soothe her. Helmut just clung tightly to Lydia's leg as he lay on the floor wondering what would come next. Would another bomb fall directly on them and crush the train?

What they were unable to see was that bombs had dropped in the ground just ahead of and behind the cars, pinning the entire train in the middle of the tunnel. They were trapped— buried alive in the oppressive darkness. The other passengers did not hide their fear that the military might not have enough men to spare to dig them out. Helmut's mind was spinning with thoughts of being trapped in the dark tomb forever. Would anyone come to save them? He didn't dare voice his questions to Lydia for fear of frightening Marlene even more.

Due to their rush to get back on the subway, Lydia had neglected to use the lavatories or to buy some food for them at the station, so the only thing they had were fresh baked buns that Hilda had given them for the trip. They had nothing to drink, which was just as well, since the train had no facilities and even if they had, they couldn't see to find them. Women cried and children, including Marlene, wailed until they were so exhausted they finally slept. Some of the men on the train did their best to find a way out, to no avail.

Lydia hummed and rocked Marlene, attempting to comfort her, as Helmut tried his best to think of something positive. Marlene had grown totally dependent on Lydia over the last few weeks of their journey, and she now clung to her mother, terrified that they would never escape from the total darkness. Helmut just sat on the floor next to his mother and said little since he knew how worried she was. He didn't want to wake Marlene or scare her by asking too many questions. Helmut's thoughts turned dark. He silently wondered if this was indeed the end of their journey—would this train car in the end, be their tomb. What if the soldiers didn't come, or couldn't get to them before they suffocated? After all there was a war raging outside so what difference did the lives of a few, poor refugees make?

Helmut's thoughts turned to America and he wondered if he would like the Americans, if he ever met one. As his mother had suggested, would the Americans turn out to be their saviors in the end? His Jewish friend, Jacob, had talked a lot about America. He and his mother hoped to travel to New York to stay with his aunt and uncle, whom he didn't really remember, since they'd immigrated there when he was so young. Helmut imagined what it might be like to travel to America someday—he'd heard grand stories about how big and open it was. No borders to cross and you could travel thousands of kilometers from one ocean to another. Maybe he'd find Jacob there. In his heart, he knew he wouldn't, but it was a comforting thought as he sat in the dark, uncertain of what might lie ahead. They had no way of telling the time or how long they'd been there—even if they'd had a watch, it would have been too dark to see it. It felt like days that they were trapped in the tunnel and the only sound from outside was the distant rumbling of more bombs.

Lydia did her best to make small talk with Helmut in an effort to keep him calm. She knew he had an imaginative mind and she wanted to keep his thoughts off the possibility they would never be rescued. She told him stories about their family and how their lineage traced back to Catherine the Great of Russia. "Catherine was of Prussian, German, and Austrian descent who married the man who would later become Emperor of all of Russia in 1762, Peter the third. But their marriage was unsuccessful and Peter took an empress consort."

"What is an empress consort Mutti? Helmut asked, confused.

"Well it's a woman who becomes like a wife to an already-married man."

"Is that legal?"

Lydia chuckled rocking Marlene who cried due to her full bladder, "Well when it comes to royalty Helmut, things that may be wrong for us commoners are accepted by the people."

"Oh, I see….like how the German Army can kill people just because they are not like us?"

"Shush," Lydia whispered, horrified that someone might have heard. "Let's not mention such things here. Let me finish my story of how Catherine helped our people. Early in Peter's reign he was very unpopular with the people however, Catherine had a very large following and support of many of those inside the palace. Only six months after Peter became Tsar of Russia, Catherine and many officials in the palace committed a coup d'état and overthrew the Tsar, to make Catherine the Empress or Tsarina of Russia."

"How could a woman do all that, Mutti?" Helmut questioned.

"It's called power, Helmut. She had gained the trust of the most powerful people, as well as the people of Russia. She ruled Russia successfully for forty-two years and did many wonderful things. One of those things was taking over the Ukraine, which had wonderful topsoil for farming and Russia needed more food to feed its people. Then she imported farmers from Germany to raise wheat, rye, alfalfa, and potatoes. Our Siewert ancestors moved to Zhitomir and along with many other Germans created a small German community, which grew to be a small city. Your Grandmother Natalie was born there, but in 1912 the Bolshevik Party took power in Russia and they didn't like the profitable Germans so they ousted them and sent them back to Germany. Some of our family moved to Prussia, but others were sent to Siberia and your Aunt Helen in America sent them food and other necessities."

"You mean they felt about Germans the way the Germans now feel about the Jews," Helmut whispered.

"Yes Helmut, the same way they felt threatened. Now....let's try to sleep so Marlene will settle down."

"Okay Mutti." Helmut was starting to understand human nature better, realizing that anyone different, or more successful, or of a different religion were considered a threat to many. He found it hard to understand how those differences could make good people outcasts to those who were more insecure.

•

Two days and nights stretched on as the passengers on the train started to give up hope of ever being rescued. Some of the men had opened the train doors and tried to get to the engineer, but their way was blocked by rubble from the cave-in. What they could ascertain; however, was that the train was blocked-in front and to the rear of them, trapping them like a lightening bug in a sealed jar. Marlene cried that she had to go to the bathroom, but Lydia insisted that she would have to continue to hold it. Helmut thought for sure his kidneys would burst if he moved, so he sat as still as he could on the floor.

On the morning of the third day the exhausted passengers heard men's voices and they realized that the soldiers had indeed come to dig them out. Many occupants of the train thanked God and the soldiers for saving them. There really was quite literally a light at the end of the tunnel. However, it took much of that morning for the men to clear the tracks so that the train could move forward and continue on to the station. When they felt the first jolt of movement, everyone cheered and cried tears of joy that they weren't going to die there underground, buried alive.

CHAPTER 8

<u>Survival – The Fall of Berlin</u>

February – May 1945 — Berlin, East Germany —
Schraplau, East Germany — Magdeburg, East Germany

When they finally arrived at the next station, although they were all stiff from sitting so long, the passengers quickly scrambled to get to the lavatories to relieve themselves. They all zealously thanked the soldiers for saving them and praised them for their sacrifice. It was a miracle they had been rescued, considering the fact that the Russians were on the city's doorstep. Knowing they would have to rebook their passage, Lydia stopped at the cafe to get her children something to drink and a nourishing breakfast since they hadn't eaten in nearly three days.

Once they had finished breakfast and washed up in the lavatories, the family rebooked their tickets to Halle with a transfer to Schraplau. Although scared they might be targeted by the bombers again, they boarded the train to Lydia's cousin, Johann Fester's, home. Exhausted from their ordeal, Helmut and Marlene slept most of the way, however Lydia was far too nervous to sleep—afraid that once she had dozed off, she wouldn't wake for their stop in Halle. Lydia had not been able to notify Johann's wife, Elfrieda, that they were coming, but she was certain that she would welcome them as family and be happy that they had survived the invasion.

Their last train ride was relatively uneventful and they finally arrived in Schraplau. With the help of a few local residents, it didn't take Lydia long to locate the Fester home, but Lydia did not receive the welcome that she had hoped for. In fact, Elfrieda was somewhat irritated when they knocked on her door in the late afternoon, unannounced.

"Lydia," exclaimed Elfrieda, looking down at the two children and their bags. "What are you doing here?"

"Well, we've just traveled hundreds of miles in Auguste's wagon and by train, escaping the Russian Army." Lydia picked up Marlene, "We were quite hoping we might stay with you until Gustav can find us."

"Oh my, that's terrible….but we don't really have much room here."

There was a long, uncomfortable moment of silence as Lydia stared imploringly at her relative. "Please, we've been on the road for so long and the children are exhausted."

"I suppose for a day or two until you can find a place to stay," Elfrieda relented and opened the door wider for them to enter.

Elfrieda allowed the family to spend the night, giving them a sparse dinner, then early the next morning she took Lydia up the hill to a small house where she banged on the door. A woman answered and Elfrieda quickly negotiated for the Siewerts to rent a room in their house. It was a small, older house with an outhouse and a pump outside for water. Helmut and Marlene slept on the floor and Lydia took the small cot in the middle of the room. Awkwardly, the room they had rented was in the center of the house, which the residents walked through to get to from the living room to the kitchen. This was, to say the least, inconvenient; however, Lydia was relieved to have a roof over their heads in a seemingly safe area that the Allied Forces didn't have sighted as one of their targets. It may not have been a major target; however, it was in the flight path of the American and British bombers. Helmut spent much of his time in Schraplau lying on his back, on the top of that hill, watching the low-flying planes on their way to bomb Berlin. He quickly learned to identify the various types of planes and the country for which they flew. Most of the residents, including Lydia and Marlene, took shelter during these raids in a limestone quarry bomb shelter. Helmut however, only went with them a few times. He preferred to lay on the hillside watching the magnificent planes fly over. His nonchalance scared his mother to death that he was so exposed to the bombers, but Helmut just argued that they would have no reason to shoot at one little boy laying on a grassy hill in a small village.

Not long after they had arrived, Helmut witnessed an unusually large number of aircraft flying overhead towards Berlin. The Allied Forces and the Red Army blitzed Berlin with three hundred fourteen air raids over a two-week period, until the end of March, leaving little remaining of the city. In mid-April the Americans arrived first in Schraplau, as Lydia had predicted. The friendly demeanor of the U.S. soldiers made the locals realize that the enemy they had feared all along was in fact their savior and nothing like the barbarians from the Russian Army.

The American envoy included just four soldiers in a Jeep, along with a few trucks carrying supplies, and an observation biplane that flew over the town. The locals were surprised at how humane and friendly the Americans were and how they did their best to help the residents of the city—providing them with food and supplies such as medicine. Helmut and a young boy named Kirk, who he'd become friendly with, talked with several of the soldiers who gave them chocolate bars to their extreme delight. It was the first time Helmut had ever eaten chocolate and the tasty treat left him in awe that the generous Americans had such delicacies to share.

Helmut was intrigued by one American solder in particular—a man with very dark skin.   He had seen these men in movies and newsreels, but never in person.   The Negro soldier climbed down from one of the trucks and came over to speak to the boys, giving them each an American penny. Helmut was awestruck.   He thanked the soldier, thrilled with the bright copper coin the soldier sergeant had placed in his hand.

Helmut reached out to shake his hand, "Hi….my name is Helmut Siewert, what's your name?"

The soldier tipped his hat at him, "Sergeant Washington, pleased to meet you, Helmut." The soldier then held out his hand to shake.

"You mean like the American President?" Helmut shook his hand vigorously, in awe.

"Yep, just like that."

Helmut studied the penny and reached out to hand it back to the officer.

"No, that's for you to keep. It's an American penny."

Helmut turned it over a few times and then put it in his pocket. "Thank you, sir!"

The sergeant gave Helmut an American military salute. Helmut smiled broadly and saluted him back with the exact same gesture.

•

On April sixteenth the Red Army surrounded Berlin in what would later be known as the 'Battle of Berlin.' By the nineteenth the situation in the city was hopeless. Hitler made his last trip from the Führerbunker to the Chancellery to award the Iron Cross to fanatical members of the Hitler Youth for bravery in fighting the Red Army. Three days later, the Führer was told that the Red Army's tanks had reached Berlin. With this news Hitler fell into a tearful rage and finally declared that Germany had indeed lost the war. He vowed that he would remain in his bunker until the end and then shoot himself rather than be captured by the Russians.

On April twenty-eighth, when he learned that his trusted leader of the SS and architect of the Holocaust, Heinrich Himmler, was negotiating surrender with Western Allies through Count Folke Bernadotte, a Swedish diplomat, Hitler grew furious. He deemed this attempt at surrender nothing less than treason and Hitler ordered that he be arrested. After midnight on the twenty-eighth, Hitler married Eva Braun in the bunker and then proceeded to dictate his last will and testament to his private secretary, Gertraud (Traudi) Junge. At 3:15 am Martin Ludwig Bormann, head of the Nazi Party Chancellery, sent a radio message to inform Hitler's hand-picked successor, Admiral Karl Donitz, of the Führer's death—he had shot himself after Eva swallowed cyanide. As per Hitler's instructions, their bodies were to be burned in the garden behind the chancellery. Berlin fell on May second and the Germans finally surrendered six days later.

Helmut and Lydia heard reports of Hitler's death on the German radio, as well as from a Soviet officer's remark, "Nothing is left of Berlin but memories." The residents of Schraplau were somber, with mixed emotions vacillating between sadness, fear, and relief that the war was finally over. They still didn't know what evil the arrival of the Russian Army might bring, but with Hitler dead, they hoped that the Red Army's soldiers would be less driven to destroy everything in their path. People hung welcome banners for the Soviets as well as white bed sheets on their lines as a sign of surrender to the Russians. The American presence gave them some measure of comfort, but all in all, their future was unknown. The Siewerts stayed in Schraplau waiting with hope that Gustav would somehow find them, if he were still alive.

On their way to Schraplau, Lydia had learned of the Yalta Conference that took place earlier in February. It was a pact that was about to severely affect the future division of Germany and the reason she felt safe waiting for Gustav in Schraplau. She had hoped that the Americans, rather than the Russians, would ultimately take charge of the town. The results of this conference held on the Crimean Peninsula by the 'Big Three'—U.S. President Franklin D. Roosevelt, Britain's Prime Minister Winston Churchill, and Soviet Premier Joseph Stalin—parceled out the post-war fate of Germany, and secured the Soviet's assistance for the continuing war in the Pacific against Japan. A formal agreement was drafted dividing Germany into four post-war occupied zones controlled by the U.S., the British, the French, and the Soviet military forces. They also divided Berlin into occupied zones, with all of Germany being demilitarized.

Across the country, the Germans released all political prisoners before the Russians arrival, since Hitler had imprisoned anyone known to be a Communist. When the Russians eventually came to Schraplau, they took over the city from the Americans, since it seemed that the U.S. soldiers had advanced too far beyond the mandates of their treaty. The residents were sorry to see them leave since the Americans had provided more for the residents of the city than the Russians and soon the town teetered on the brink of starvation.

Even though Lydia applied for ration cards, it didn't help the family very much, since the town had simply run out of food. There was little or nothing to buy at the butcher, the bakery, or the grocer. When the Russians arrived, they pretty much stripped the town of anything of value including the food supply and they cut off all communications, which would prevent Gustav from contacting them. The Soviets even removed much of the metal and wood from the train tracks heading west, as well as any equipment from factories and all materials were sent back to Russia. Everyone in town was afraid of the soldiers and worried that they might actually starve.

Lydia, Helmut, and Marlene stayed in their rented room for several months until miraculously, Gustav arrived at their door late one afternoon. He had escaped from the prisoner of war camp in Sachsen-Anhalt, wearing his German Army uniform and weighing only one hundred thirty-five pounds of his original two hundred eighty.

When Lydia answered the knock at the door she was overjoyed to see Gustav standing there, although it took her a moment to recognize her husband at half his stature from when she had last laid eyes on him. "HELMUT! MARLENE!" she shouted as she threw her arms around him. "Hurry! Papa is here!"

"Papa, Papa!" Marlene squealed as she ran to Gustav and hugged him as he scooped her up in his arms.

Helmut ran to the door, "You found us!" Helmut smiled but hesitated in hugging his father. They had never had that kind of relationship, although Helmut desperately wanted to give him a welcoming hug since he was so happy to see him. "How on earth did you know where we were?"

"A little bird told me Helmut," Gustav laughed.

"But how did you get here?" questioned Lydia; looking at his injured leg and the walking stick he leaned on.

"I walked all one hundred seventy-seven kilometers from Sachsen-Anhalt, mostly at night."

"Oh my goodness, come you must lie down!" Lydia insisted as she helped him into their room, where she sat him down on her bed.

It was an amazing reunion now that the family was back together again. Gustav told them stories that night of how, even though he was half blind from an experimental drug he was given for his leg injury, he had still managed to walk all the way to Schraplau. He had been able to escape since the POW camps were nothing more than field tents with barbed wire fencing.

Gustav later informed Elfrieda that her husband, August, had been captured at Stalingrad, but he had no way of knowing if or when he would be released. Elfrieda was beside herself with the uncertainly of not knowing if she would ever see her husband again.

●

The Siewert family was Baptist, but there was no organized church in Schraplau that they could attend, so instead they attended meetings held in various homes around town. In fact, being Baptist was a little frowned on by the predominantly Lutheran and Catholic community. Gustav worked with their makeshift Baptist congregation, becoming the choir director, and Lydia played guitar. She had been teaching Helmut to play, but she knew that he needed to find his own guitar in order to practice in his spare time. Helmut's full-time job was to find food for the family, which was no easy feat since the small twenty by twenty foot grocery had little to offer. It meant standing in line for hours to buy anything. Basic staples such as salt, sugar and grain were especially hard to find.

Even though food was scarce, they stayed in Schraplau, for several more months, until Gustav felt it was safe for them to travel and the family left on the first train out for the town of Magdeburg—situated on the Elbe River, where his brother Otto lived with his wife, Ester.   Somehow, Gustav had learned of his brother's imprisonment by the American Army in Italy and he decided that they would go to stay with Ester and her elderly mother, who needed help. As had been the case with Elfrieda, the family was unable to notify Ester that they were coming and they arrived with no notice. They received a more welcome greeting from Ester, who was grateful to learn that her husband was alive and that he might be released sometime in the near future to return home. She invited them to stay, however their living conditions were not a great deal better than they'd been in Schraplau. At least the house was a little larger and on a farm where they could grow their own food. Ester worked at a large estate in the nearby town of Domersleben supervising the children of nobility, so she would live there during the week.   Food was short in Magdeburg, so the family made the decision to move further west in the autumn to Domersleben since Ester had found a small house for them to rent.

Gustav learned that the Communists there were dividing large farms into twenty-acre parcels—designated to be given to refugees in Domersleben. It was a small town resembling something from the Middle Ages, with a stonewall surrounding the entire town. After they were there a while, they rented a very old, run-down, two-bedroom farmhouse that had only a cooking stove for heat. The problem was that there was no coal to be had anywhere in the area. Not only was it Helmut's job to find food for the family, he now had to gather wood for the fire to keep them warm. However, all the other residents also needed firewood, so there was little available for Helmut to cut and collect. To make matters worse, the Russians forbade the residents to cut the trees so instead they simply stripped all the branches from them, leaving not much of the tree besides the trunk. Thankfully, Helmut was light and agile, as well as a good climber, so he could get to the best branches at the top of the trees. Although Gustav was still disabled from his unhealed leg injury and his failing eyesight, he managed to work for the Russians on one of the nearby farms. They made him carry heavy sacks of grain up two stories for storage in the grain lofts. It was a backbreaking, all-day job, but he had no choice since they still didn't have their own farm. Although there was an abundance of grain, the Russians never shared it with any of the refugee families. If any of the grain spilled, Gustav would do his best to sneak a handful into his pocket for food to be eaten later.

•

Like many towns in Germany, a 'Baron' of German nobility had owned most of the land in Domersleben for centuries. It had been the custom for centuries that in return for a small parcel of land to work, a farmer must to allow the baron the first night of matrimony with the farmer's new wife. The Russians had taken over most these farmlands when they arrived and either killed or evicted the majority of the wealthy land barons so they could divide the land into smaller farms for the refugees. Helmut's family was given lottery tickets for land and they pulled two parcels totaling twenty acres, in different locations, a few kilometers outside of town. They were also given an ox for plowing, two cows for milk, a female goose to start raising geese for meat, a chicken for eggs to eat, and a pig to fatten and supply towards their food quota required by the Russians. They were also required to sell grain to the state—both wheat and rye in the winter and the summer. Once the farmers gave their quota of food, they were allowed to keep what remained. However, if they didn't provide their required donation, they were punished and penalized by being denied food.

When they first arrived, the total town population was only sixteen hundred to eighteen hundred residents so it was a little easier to find food for the family. However, with the influx of fleeing refugees, the population exploded to nearly six thousand almost overnight, putting extreme pressure on the town's resources. There was little food to eat and survival was a constant challenge, forcing people to scavenge anything they could find to feed their families. They even started raising sugar beets to grind down and cook to make sugar and grow poppies for poppy seeds to grind to make oil for baking. They applied for food stamps, called Lebensmittle: Karten— once again they meant nothing since there was little or no food available to purchase from the town's vendors.

During the day Helmut worked in the fields cutting down weeds—often getting criticized by his father for not doing it right. At night the family sent Helmut out with a cart to steal heads of cabbage and carrots from neighboring farms. This became a nightly ritual especially around harvest season. He was nearly caught several times and chased on horseback by irate farmers wielding lanterns and pitchforks. Luckily, Helmut was swifter and more nimble than the older farmers, who suffered from failing eyesight in the darkness. Helmut would simply wait in the woods until the farmer had gone to bed and then return for his cart full of vegetables. The next day, Lydia would use his stolen booty to make a kettle-full of hearty soup for the family.

At the end of the week's work, Saturday night was bath night for the entire family—Helmut having to help pump the water and heat it on the stove. Their bath was a large round galvanized tub and Helmut was unfortunately always the last in line to have his bath. By then, the water was quite cold and dirty with the grime of four others floating on the top. Helmut had decided that it was unfair for Marlene to get her bath before him, so one Saturday he decided to voice his opinion, "Mutti, why is it the Marlene gets to bathe before me? After all, she is younger and doesn't do any work around here? I'm the one carrying most of the water."

"Well Helmut, she's a young lady and you need to learn that ladies always come first."

"But why--"

"--no buts Helmut," Lydia curtly cut him off before he could finish his thought. "Ask your father to teach you about how to treat women. It will be one of the most important things you ever learn in this life," and with that the conversation was abruptly terminated.

Underwear was only changed once a week, so it only required that Helmut own two pair, so he had a clean one while the other was being washed. He realized however, that his mother and sister had an extra pair that allowed them to change them in the middle of the week and that, he thought, was another unfair advantage that females had over the men. Helmut realized that maybe it was time to have a man-to-man talk with his father about such things if Gustav was willing. But, once again, his father was not very forthcoming with information about women's undergarments.

●

Gustav's sister, Helen, had moved to America to live in Milwaukee, Wisconsin back in the thirties and she generously sent the family routine packages of food and coffee as often as she could. Since coffee was not grown anywhere in Germany it was considered a very rare commodity, so rather than using it for themselves they traded it on the black market in return for a guitar for Helmut and a horse and wagon to plow the fields. Their ox, Miceof, had always been very uncooperative and difficult to work with even when prodded with a long stick that had a nail on the end. Because of his resistance to work, they always came up short on grain for themselves after their quota was paid. The ox however, came in handy when they traded him in, since they managed to reach their meat quota and then some for an entire year. Helmut felt guilty about Miceof's demise, but even at his young age, he already understood that it was just business and a matter of their survival. Besides, he was thrilled to finally have a horse since he loved working with them back on his grandfather's farm. He took on total responsibility for taking care of their new steed, Heidi. He rode her as often as he could, especially in the winter months, always using the excuse that he was exercising her.

A few weeks after their arrival, Gustav's father, also named Gustav, and his Jewish mother, Natalie, arrived in a wagon to live with them, making it even harder to find enough food

for the family. Soon after they arrived, however Helmut's grandfather developed gangrene from frostbite in his feet and died
from the infection, since they had no medicine or doctors to treat
him. The closest doctor was more than three kilometers from
town and there was little money to pay for any form of medical
treatment.

On February 1st, 1946 Lydia gave birth to an unplanned,
baby boy named Dieter, so Natalie stayed on with them after her
husband's death to assist Lydia in caring for her newborn. It gave
Natalie a new reason for living after her husband's passing she so
enjoyed taking care of the newest member of their family. Unfortunately, Lydia had no breast milk due to her own poor diet and
Helmut was sent out to beg the surrounding farmers for milk to
feed his new brother. He didn't like the idea of begging, but he
knew he had no choice since the life of his baby brother hung in
the balance. Gustav and Helmut built a small crib from one-by-
two wood scraps they found and they filled the cradle with hay.
Lydia then covered Dieter with a towel to keep him warm. Having a little brother thrilled Helmut and he helped his mother as
much as he could with the household chores, but he was usually
busy after school helping his father with his chores on the farm.

CHAPTER 9

<u>The Bitter Taste of Socialism</u>

Autumn 1946 - 1952 — Domersleben, East Germany

Once the family was settled in Domersleben and dire hunger was no longer the only thing on their minds, Helmut started fourth grade and Marlene started first. The local children disliked Helmut as well as the other refugee students, since their presence only added to the poverty and lack of food in their small town. Their classrooms grew so large that sometimes they were forced to hold sessions outside. Helmut's earlier study had been in a more advanced school, so it created competition and tension between him and the other students in his class. He was tall and skinny with a shaved head and the tougher and larger boys often picked on him, forcing him to fight his way through primary school.

One day five children from the same family circled around Helmut taunting him with jeers and names. "Hey baldy," shouted the largest boy, Reinhart. "Why don't you go back to where you came from? You're probably Russian, aren't you?"

"I am not Russian, I'm from West Prussia," insisted Helmut.

"Same thing!" shouted another boy.

"No, it's not I'm full-blooded German," continued Helmut turning to walk away.

Suddenly, the four boys and one girl attacked Helmut, kicking him with their wooden shoes. The girl even removed her shoes and hit him over the head with them. Helmut struggled as a loner for four years in school, but eventually managed to make three fast friends, Manfred, Guenter, and Eckhard. All three boys were also from East Prussia, so they felt as if they had something in common—camaraderie.

A year and a half after the Siewerts settled in Domersleben, Helmut's Uncle, Emiel Grapentien—Lydia's brother, arrived at their home with his four daughters, Lisebet, Hilde, Imgard and Elfriede. Emiel brought with him the terrible news that his and Lydia's mother had remained behind on her farm and had been captured by the Russians. They had also confiscated all the family farmland. Lydia was beside herself with grief, but there was little she could do at that point to help her mother. Ultimately, no one would ever learn her fate and where she had been taken.

In addition, Emiel told the gruesome tale of his wife and fifth daughter being captured by the Russians. They had lagged behind the wagon train, having returned home in East Prussia to get more possessions during the evacuation, and were overtaken by the soldiers. All the women had been violently raped multiple times and his wife, Otiela, and daughter, also named Otiela, had tragically lost their legs at the knees, when an artillery shell hit the front of their wagon. His wife and daughter had died from their injuries after being gang-raped by the Russian soldiers while bleeding to death. Emiel eventually found his four living daughters in a nursing home in East Germany, after he was released from a prisoner of war camp. The four girls were moved into the Siewert family's attic with Helmut. The two older girls, Lisebet and Elfriede went to school with Helmut, but only Elfriede was in his class.

Elfriede was six months older than Helmut and very bright. She became extremely competitive with him in school, pushing him to excel in class. At first they were somewhat estranged, due to the competition between them, but in time they became close friends. She served as a great inspiration for Helmut and inspired him to broaden his scholastic skills, ultimately pushing him to the top of his class. Helmut found Elfriede extremely attractive—slim with fair skin and thick, dark brown hair, but she he was driven by her need to prove herself smarter than Helmut. It wasn't until Helmut decided to give in and let her feel superior to him that they finally began to bond. In the summer they would take their lunch into the field and lay in the sun to share their food.

After a few weeks, Emiel left his daughters with the Helmut's family and he crossed the border into West Germany. The girls remained with the Siewerts for a year and a half and helped Gustav and Helmut as much as they could on the farm. Eventually, their father sent them money to cross the border and join him in West Germany, where he had found work. In the west, the girls could work for four times the amount of pay as they could make in East Germany. Helmut found it hard to say goodbye to Elfriede, since he'd not only become fast friends with his cousin, but he was also quite smitten with her.

•

By the age of twelve years old, Helmut had greatly excelled in class and was smarter than most of the other children in school, to the point of being asked to tutor some of the other children in his class as there were three different grades in one classroom. He liked school, especially math, geography, and history, but his advanced skills sometimes made him unpopular with the other children. None of that mattered to Helmut, however since his friend Jacob had been the one to inspire him with his knowledge of the world. He had triggered Helmut's interest in broadening his horizons and he now thought well beyond the borders of Germany.

Helmut not only did well at school, but he also worked hard helping his mother and father with household and farming chores, and still managed to make several close friends from school. One was a boy named Guenter, who he did sport with after school, but he was especially fond of a pretty girl named Giesala, whom he walked home everyday after school.

Helmut's school day consisted of five hours of classes. In addition to the mandatory studies, he had to study three years of Russian, German, and music— his instrument of choice being the guitar. He was rarely in trouble until the day that he and his friends made cigarettes out of some local plants and smoked them, leaving the stench of smoke on his clothing and his hair. The moment he arrived home and his mother smelled the evidence of his sinful ways; it prompted one of the few whippings that she ever inflicted upon him.

•

In the autumn, after the harvest, Helmut and his friends would go to the fields to hunt for wild hamsters. They would set round traps in the hamster hole effectively trapping the rodents for food. After skinning, cleaning, and frying them they would eat the tasty treat for extra protein. The industrious hamsters came with an additional bonus—down inside their burrows they stored up to fifty pounds of grain from the fields. The boys would dig out this secret cache of grain and use it for food for themselves and their families, since it was not reported to the government. Helmut also continued his nightly raids, during harvest season, for peas, cabbage, carrots, and tomatoes, reasoning that his family needed it more than the farmers needed the money in their pockets. They also harvested the poppy seeds grown in the fields to make oil for cooking. By selling some of the extra oil they processed, they eventually made enough money to buy an electric grinder for the seeds. Their house was modern enough to have electric power, but their only source of heat was the ornate tiled coal stove, which they would damper at night to keep the house warm. As before, there was never any coal available to burn in the stove, so that meant that gathering wood for it was included in Helmut's daily chores.

•

At the age of thirteen, Helmut and his father started nightly treks to take the train to a stop near the border and then they covertly walked through the woods across the border into West Germany. They navigated minefields with extreme caution and snuck past armed guards at the checkpoint. Their mission was to purchase smoked fish, butter, chocolate, coffee, and oranges, some of which they sold on the black market for extra income. Gustav's brother, Herbert, was a West German border guard and he would inform them when he would be on duty assuring them that he would turn a blind eye to their comings and goings. He also informed them when there were distractions in the village, resulting in fewer guards on duty. One night Helmut and Gustav were caught crossing back over the border with their food. There was a full moon that night and the short Russian guard on duty at the East German checkpoint spotted them. He shouted demanding they stop or he would shoot, but Gustav kept going. Helmut turned to see the guard's rifle trained on them and he grabbed his father's arm, with an iron grip, insisting, "Stop! Father, he WILL shoot us!"

"We have to run, Helmut!" Gustav insisted, resisting his son's pleas— trying to pull away, but Helmut gripped him tighter.

"Stop! I don't really want to be shot in the back! You can't see, but he has his gun pointed at us."

Gustav paused looking back at the guard—then at his son, "I'm afraid that what they will do to us may be worse than getting shot." With that, Gustav dropped his bundle and held up his arms in surrender.

Helmut and Gustav were promptly arrested at gunpoint and taken to an old, abandoned house for questioning. Their passports and the food were seized and they were held prisoners in the derelict house with boarded up windows, and no source of light. For three days and three nights Helmut and Gustav were certain that their captors would never release them—they just sat there in the dark wondering what fate awaited them. Would they be sent to prison in Russia, or would they be shot for breaking the law and crossing the border for illegal goods? It was the first time that Helmut had really gotten to know his father as they talked, trying to distract their minds from their precarious situation and impending sentencing. Their worst fear was that the family would have to pay for their crime. By the third day they began wondering if anyone would actually come back for them and their imaginations ran wild with thoughts of starving to death in their dark prison. They tried their best to break down the door, but it proved impossible, as they had no tools with which to work. On the third day of their imprisonment, the door opened and the guard entered the house carrying his rifle, backlit by the bright daylight. Helmut and Gustav squinted watching him and held their breath. Maybe they would be shot right there on the spot. Instead, to their astonishment, the man simply returned their passports with a stern warning, "Don't do it again!" He pointed his rifle to the door indicating that they should leave. Father and son looked at each other wondering if this was simply a trap. Would they be shot in the back for escaping if they followed his order? The guard insisted again and they hesitantly walked through the door.

Once outside, they were relieved they were still alive as they walked back to the main road. Silently, they thanked God and their lucky stars that they hadn't been shot in the back and they were free to leave with no further punishment. After they arrived at the train station and cleaned themselves up, hunger made a bold decision for them. That very night they returned across the border for more food. Hunger, it seemed, was a much more powerful motivator than fear. Despite their unsettling experience, Helmut and his father managed to strengthen their relationship through their frightening event and they continued to cross the border at least six more times on their black market smuggling missions.

Helmut shared some of the food, but nothing of its origin, with his friends—splitting an orange or a chocolate bar between three of them. He would never share the source of the food's origin—only allude to the fact that his aunt in America often sent them care packages and his friends would in turn help him sell coffee and buy necessities for the farm.

Helmut was greatly overworked, between school, his farm chores and the responsibility of his sister and brother's care.

Marlene attended school in the mornings and Gustav made it Helmut's job to look out for her in the afternoons. If anything ever harmed or threatened his favorite child, his father would punish him for allowing it to happen. Helmut often took Marlene to the farm in the afternoon and she would play in the dirt while Helmut worked. He was frustrated by this responsibility, since his sister was extremely clumsy and managed to fall flat on her face often, as if she had no arms with which to catch herself when she tripped.   So each time she managed another tumble, Helmut would receive another punishment for his lack of supervision, since she always seemed to do some sort of damage to her face. He grew resentful of this unwanted responsibility, even though he loved his siblings. He just wished that his sister could be a bit less careless when it came to walking.

Since giving birth to Marlene, Lydia had suffered from blood clots in her legs. She often blamed Marlene for her worsening health issues—many times feeling too exhausted to even take care of her daughter. Like Gustav, she often transferred the responsibility for Marlene's wellbeing to Helmut. On the few days Lydia felt up to it, she allowed Marlene to invite her friends from school over to play and even made them sandwiches or cake as a treat. On those days, Helmut looked forward to time off from his childcare responsibilities. Since Helmut was Lydia's favorite, she did what she could to provide him some relief whenever she felt up to it.

•

When Natalie moved to Domersleben she brought her spinning wheel with her and was able to make wool from the sheep they raised for meat, whenever they sheared them. In Helmut's spare time, Natalie taught him to spin the wool. Just in case something should happen to her, she knew that someone in the family should also learn the craft. The wool they produced served to provide a little extra income for the family, not to mention servicing their own needs. To supplement their food supply for their growing family, Helmut and his mother also started raising rabbits to eat. It took some time for Helmut to get used to killing and cleaning them, but after a time, it simply became a part of their survival. The hardest part was that Marlene grew attached to the bunnies and gave them all names, so they had to pretend they had simply found them new homes when their time came. Helmut even tried his hand at raising geese, but since they only laid an egg once every few days and he had no way of knowing if it was fertilized, he grew frustrated. After having the goose sit on multiple eggs for up to three weeks only to find that none of them were fertilized, he gave up the poultry business and ate the goose. It was a delicious week's worth of meals even if it hadn't paid off as a successful business enterprise.

The local farms had many cherry and plum tree orchards and Helmut's teacher would enlist him and his classmates to assist with harvesting the fruit. Due to the fact that the boys would be allowed to eat what they wanted and take a basket of fruit home to their families, his teacher always had more volunteers than needed. When Helmut brought the basket of fruit home, his father ate the lion's share, including every cherry, pits and all. Luckily, Helmut had already gotten his fill while working in the fields, but he felt bad that his siblings had been cheated of this special treat that only came once a year.

The students did not get summers off, so it left little time for Helmut to have time off for himself. At the end of eighth grade, he worked even more as a teacher's assistant tutoring younger children in math and geography, two subjects in which he excelled. Helmut worked hard that year, spending five hours a day in school as well as doing an hour of homework, not to mention working in the fields for four to five hours a day. However, he did find time to date one of his students, Margie, a dark-haired girl who was a Domersleben native. They dated for a while until she broke up with him—later wanting to get back together, but Helmut had eyes on several other girls by then and turned her down.

Since eighth grade was the highest level of education available in Domersleben, Helmut went to work in a full-time apprenticeship just before his fifteenth birthday. He was given only three options for an apprenticeship—farming, working in the uranium mine, or learning the trade of bricklaying. Helmut chose bricklaying since his three best friends, Eckhard, Guenter, and Manfred were already working as mason apprentices. They worked nine-hour days, four days a week, and went to school to learn their trade, as well as high school classes two days a week in a different town. Helmut walked or rode the family bike to and from his classes. His teacher, Mr. Heinrich, taught him a great deal about drawing and reading plans, as well as how to run his own business. He became good friends with Mr. Heinrich and they would often play table tennis together after class. It was the only real social activity that Helmut permitted himself to indulge in since his time was so limited.

Helmut was required to go to church on Sundays, so he didn't find much time to be a teenage boy and hang out with his friends. There was one girl, however, that he went out with a few times, but she was several years younger than him. Because of the age difference, he didn't see her for long, but he became quite smitten with another very special girl in his class named, Anna. In fact, he even thought, maybe it was true love. The problem was, she was the daughter of his soon-to-be employer, Mr. Fredkin, a master bricklayer.

Helmut began his apprenticeship with Mr. Fredkin, who was a tough, but fair man. But where his daughter, Anna, was concerned, he was very strict when it came to her dating blue-collar workers, especially the ones that worked for him. Helmut no longer saw Anna in class, but he did have the chance to see her on occasion after work. When Helmut tried asking his boss about taking his daughter on a date, Mr. Fredkin simply replied, "Helmut, you're a good worker, but be sure to keep your place on this job."

"Excuse me, sir?"

"Let me make this very, very clear. You are never to date my daughter. And you are never to bring up the subject again. Do you understand?"

"Yes Sir," Helmut answered with a heavy tone of disappointment in his voice, having just been given the very same order his father always gave. "Never bring up the subject again."

So Helmut refrained from pursuing the subject further. He just hoped his boss would never find out that he had already gone out with his daughter several times. After all, he loved his job and learning a trade and he didn't want to do anything to jeopardize that, as much as he liked Anna. He also hoped that this skill would allow him to not only build beautiful houses one day, but also be paid well for his work. He dreamed of a time in the future that he would actually be able to build his own home. Maybe then he would be worthy of Mr. Fredkin's daughter.

Most importantly, Helmut really enjoyed being able to work with his three best friends. Eckhard unfortunately had been injured on a roofing job by falling two-and-a-half stories. He sustained a badly broken leg, as well as many other contusions. Helmut also fell, however a pear tree that broke his fall to the ground caught him. As a result of his injuries, Eckhard was forced to complete his apprenticeship at a later date, but Manfred and Guenter completed their apprenticeships and joined the bricklayers union. Once the boys belonged to the union they were given the option to attend university in Halle. The possibility of a higher education really tempted Helmut, but there was one catch—at the age of eighteen he would be required to join the Communist Party.

After two and a half years of hard work, Helmut graduated with a certificate as a journeyman bricklayer and received a letter of recommendation from his employer. The big question he now faced—would he be willing to join the Party when he turned eighteen?

Years had passed, but economically little changed in Eastern Germany. Economic recovery in the rest of Europe was also slow, but in 1948 the Marshall Plan, or the European Recovery

Program, was provided by America. The Marshall Plan had in-jected more than fifteen billion dollars, over four years towards the rebuilding efforts in Western Europe. It was designed to reestablish industry, trade, cities, and the general infrastructure of West Germany, which had been so badly destroyed by the war. It was also designed to help halt the spread of communism across Europe. Unfortunately, the aid didn't reach Soviet-controlled Eastern Germany and the financial situation there had not im-proved, and neither had the finances of the Siewert family. Hel-mut felt little hope of a lucrative career if he remained in Domer-sleben.

It was then in the spring of 1952 that Helmut made a life-changing decision—escape East Germany to the West, where he could live and work in a newly formed Democracy. On May 23, 1949 the West had emerged out of the rubble of the war with the formation of the Federal Republic of Germany—a new experi-ment of democracy. In the East, the Soviet Union had established the German Democratic Republic in Frankfurt, ruled by the So-cialist Unity Party of Germany. Even though Helmut had been offered a scholarship at the University of Halle for a higher edu-cation, he made the decision that he was totally unwilling to join the Communist Party. He wasn't certain how he would get there, but he set his mind to find a way to escape the control of social-ism and communism. He also knew that because he would be

forced to join the Communist Party the day he turned eighteen—
the clock was ticking—that was only six months away.

PART II

ESCAPING COMMUNISIM

1952 – 1954 — West Germany

CHAPTER 10

<u>Escape to the West – A Confession</u>

1952 – 1954 — Domersleben, East Germany — Neubüten-stadt, West Germany — Warpe, West Germany

Helmut had to break the news to his parents that he had made the decision to move to the West and he knew it wouldn't be easy to convince them that it was in the family's best interest. One night when the whole family was around the dinner table he broached the subject.

"I've made a decision," Helmut announced confidently.

"You haven't decided to join the Communist Party have you?" asked Gustav, concerned.

"No….just the opposite," Helmut shook his head. "I've decided to move to West Germany to work as a bricklayer. "I can make four times as much money there."

The family just looked at him in shock.

"Oh Helmut, you can't leave us," Lydia almost started to cry.

"What about your income for the household?" questioned Gustav, quite worried, knowing he was unable to work, due to his leg injury.

"That's the whole point. Since you are unable to work, I can send more to you from West Germany than I'm making now."

Gustav pondered this for a moment. "Point made....I guess then you can become the family's primary breadwinner."

"Of course," Helmut said relieved. "And once I get settled there and can afford a place for all of us to live, you will be able to join me there."

Gustav looked at Lydia and patted her hand. She was still on the brink of tears.

"It's for the best, Mutti. We can have a better life there," Helmut assured his mother.

Lydia just nodded, unhappy with the thought of her eldest leaving the nest.

"Well then, it's settled. When do you plan to leave?" asked Gustav.

"As soon as possible since on my birthday I'll be forced to join the Party."

"Well then, I'll make arrangements with my brother at the border."

And with that, Helmut's future was decided.

Marlene was in school and old enough to help her mother with the household chores as well as care for Dieter. But she was also an apprentice in a small food store in Domersleben. Unfortunately, her pay was so little it hardly made any difference to help the family. Of course, Dieter was only seven and much too young to earn an income. So, all told, Helmut knew the burden to provide for his family lay squarely on his shoulders.

Helmut's plan was to go to live with his Aunt Auguste and Uncle Johann and their sons Wilfried and Gerhard, as well as his grandmother, Natalie, who had moved to Warpe a few years prior from East Germany. He was excited to see his cousins again, since he had grown so close to Wilfried on their trek. By living with them, Helmut would have to pay little or no rent and could send as much as possible to his family in East Germany. Helmut's father liked the idea—this would entirely relieve him of the financial burden for his family.

Thanks to his uncle, Helmut managed to get a permit to take the train from Domersleben to the border near Helmstedt,

West Germany. Helmstedt was occupied by the Americans, the French, and the British on the west side of the border, while armed German and Russian patrols strictly controlled the east side of the border.   Once aboard the train his papers were not re-checked and Helmut was able to ride as close as two stops before the West German border.   Under the cover of darkness, Helmut crossed the border on foot the night before May first. Gustav had learned from his brother, Herbert, who worked as a guard on the west side of the border, that there would be fewer guards pa-trolling the night before May Day due to their celebrations. Once across Helmut went directly to the border patrol on the west side and asked to be taken to his uncle. Thanks to Herbert, he was not only welcomed, but also given a ride to the town of Neubüeten-stadt. By that point, nearly two million East Germans had es-caped to the West in search of a better life, since they were invit-ed and welcomed to immigrate there by the West German gov-ernment.

Helmut lived in Neubüetenstedt, West Germany for three months working two and a half kilometers away as a bricklayer by day in Helmstedt. At night he dug up graves to move bodies from a cemetery for an ambitious coal mining operation, so that they could mine the coal underneath the gravesites. It was Hel-mut's job to relocate the bodies and the gravestones, but first he and his co-worker had to dig the new graves. They would then exhume the old graves and place the crumbling remains of the corpses into wooden coffins, then rebury them in the new gravesites in a different area. It was a gruesome job and his first co-worker only lasted a few nights. That man was quickly replaced by another who had a stronger stomach, or, an empty one––hungry for the extra pay. After what he'd seen at the end of the war, Helmut made peace with the fact that at least these poor souls were being given a respectful place to rest. So many who had been slain by the Russians were simply left in the fields as carrion for the birds and wolves to scavenge.

Helmut went to live with Auguste, Johann, Natalie, and his cousins, but two months after he arrived, Wilfried and Gerhard immigrated to Wisconsin in America. It was more complicated for Auguste and Johann to get their visas, since they were born in Russia and America was very concerned about allowing potential Communists into the country. So, the boys went alone to live with their Aunt Helen Deblitz in Milwaukee, who sponsored them and sent them the money needed for their trip to the U.S. Once they were established and working, the boys would be able to help Helen bring their parents over.

Auguste and Johann eventually applied for their visas and they were required to provide three things—money for the flight over, evidence of housing in America, and proof of funds for living expenses. Eventually, their many trips to Hamburg to apply for immigration to the U.S. paid off and the two were also given their visas to travel to America. Unfortunately, because Auguste and Johann had built their house on leased land, they were unable to sell it, so they gave it to Helmut to use while he was living in Warpe.

After their successful departure to America, Helmut began making his own plans to follow suit. He had landed himself a good-paying job as a bricklayer and he sent a few hundred marks to his parents every month as he had promised. The rest he saved for his eventual trip to America. At night Helmut read as many books in German as he could acquire, since he still didn't speak English. He read books such as *Ben Hur*, and *Gone with the Wind* as well as many Native American stories to help him learn the history and background of the United States. He spoke 'high German,' which he hoped would help him in the predominantly German community of Milwaukee when he eventually immigrated there. But, he also knew that to succeed in business in America he would have to learn to speak English very well.

•

It took nearly a year before Helmut was able to send his family enough money for them to escape East Germany and make their way to Warpe. Since there was already housing for them in Johann's home, it made it possible for the family to live there on Helmut's income. For the next two years, Helmut worked very hard at his job and managed to save his money for his trip to America. He was a skilled bricklayer and made a very good salary for such a young man. He knew how to layout buildings and basements better than any of the other masons, which put him in demand. As well as he was doing there, he knew he could make even more money if he could become a foreman in America. So, Helmut decided it was time to contact his Aunt Helen in Milwaukee and set his own immigration plans to America into motion.

Most of his days at work were fairly repetitious and predictable, however one day when Helmut was starting on a new project to add a new room to a restaurant in Warpe, he picked up his tools and followed his co-workers through a bedroom in order to get to the new addition. To his shock and surprise there were three naked adults intertwined in bed—two men and a woman still sound asleep. Embarrassed that they had intruded into their private sanctum, Helmut averted his eyes, so as to avoid staring at the unusual threesome. It was later that his co-workers explained that the woman's husband had been drafted to fight at the Eastern Front and she had received word that he had died in battle. A few years went by and the woman, being alone and broke took another man to live with her, assuming she was a widow. Years after the man moved into her house, the woman's husband simply showed up one day in the pink of heath. Although in shock, his wife was thrilled to see him and the three had come to an amicable, yet unusual understanding—they would all live together, making it a two-income household.   A solution that worked for all, except maybe for the woman whom looked very tired. Helmut was amazed that one woman could possibly keep both men happy since they both seemed have smiles on their faces. The three were often seen riding around town—three on one bicycle with one man pedaling, the woman on the handlebars and the second man on the rear luggage rack.

•

Shortly after the Siewerts' arrival in Warpe, Lydia's sister, Emilie Dombrowski, who lived in Delmenhorst, contacted Lydia, inviting them for a visit. The family road their bicycles the seventeen kilometers to her home and decided that they liked the area far better than Warpe. While riding through the countryside, they came across numerous vacant lots for sale and Emilie talked them into buying one for 800 marks of Helmut's money *(the equivalent of two hundred to three hundred US dollars at the time)*. He and his father decided they would build a house, which Helmut intended to put in his name; however, Gustav had a different plan— he demanded that Helmut put the new house in Gustav's name.

Helmet and his father started building the two-room house, then dismantled and moved Johann's house from Warpe, using the materials to build a kitchen and an outhouse. Unfortunately, Helmut had to use the money he was saving for his trip to America to buy the supplies needed for their new home. He knew this would delay his immigration to America, but he felt an obligation to his family to be sure they had a comfortable place to live. Their new house did not have the modern convenience of indoor plumbing, or running water, so they dug a well with an outdoor hand pump for water. They splurged and purchased a coal stove for each room and installed a number of windows to make the house bright. The last and most important addition was to plant a vegetable garden, so they could produce some food for themselves.

It was during their work on the new home in Delmenhorst, that Gustav finally made a confession to Helmut. "Now that the war is over and we are free of the Communists, I need to tell you that my mother, Natalie, is Jewish. I knew that with the rounding up of Jews to be sent to concentration camps, my mother and possibly me and my siblings would be swept up in the Nazi net of ethnic cleansing. So I took care of it."

"But why didn't you ever tell me this?" questioned Helmut, suddenly realizing why his father had refused to explain the reason he was not allowed to see his friend Jacob. "That's why you wouldn't let me play with Jacob, isn't it?"

Gustav nodded, "Your association with a Jew could have caused our entire family to risk our standing with the German government and the Nazi Party."

Gustav explained how he had forged documents for his mother when he worked at the German Administration Office in Bischofswerder. Thanks to his government job, Gustav had access to the official Hitler stamp, so he made up a signature on her passport and stamped the documents to show that she was of pure German descent. It was the first time they had talked about Gustav's knowledge of concentration camps, a topic that had been totally off limits when they were in Bischofswerder, or anywhere in East Germany for that matter.

His father's confession surprised Helmut. Not so much the fact that he had broken the law to protect and save his family, but that he now trusted his son enough to confide in him and finally tell him the truth about their heritage. Helmut was quite grateful for not only the chance his father took in breaking German law, but also his honesty. His father was finally starting to treat him like a beloved son and he suddenly saw an entirely different side of Gustav. He realized how brave he had been taking this great risk by forging official documents and he was thankful.

Had he been found out, it would have meant certain death for Gustav and Natalie. Had he not taken this chance, the entire family might have ended up disappearing in the middle of the night, just like Jacob and his mother—never to be heard from again.

•

It was around this time that Helmut started dating several attractive young women. He could have easily had his pick, since he was tall, handsome and successful, but the one he liked best was Helga Kneiding. She was a very pretty nursing student close to his age. She also attended his Baptist church and like Helmut, hoped to immigrate to America when she finished school. She wanted to join Helmut on his trip to Hamburg to apply to immigrate to the U.S., but she had no sponsor. Helmut would have to immigrate there first and then send for her after earning enough money to pay her way. He continued to live in the house he and his father had built for a year, while working as a bricklayer and continuing to apply in Hamburg for his visa to go to America. One day he decided it was time to have a serious talk with Helga.

"Helga, I think we should get married before I leave for the U.S."

Helga paused a moment before answering, "I really want to marry you Helmut, but I think we should wait until I get there. It will be the new start of our new life together."

"But it would be easier for you to immigrate there if we are already married."

"I know....but I'm not ready to leave my family and I want to finish my nursing school."

"But you can finish your schooling there. I will pay for it."

"What if you should get there and decide you want an American wife?"

"That would never happen Helga I love you and I want to marry you....now!"

But, to his great disappointment, Helga refused to budge on the subject.

It took Helmut a total of six trips to Hamburg to fill out applications, testify, and be interviewed for his visa. The fact that he'd been born in East Germany made it even more difficult, as U.S. Senator Joseph McCarthy was hell-bent on keeping Communists out of America. The Red Scare, known as McCarthyism, caused criminal investigations and hearings in an effort to expose Communists working in America intent on infiltrating the U.S.

government.   All told it took Helmut two years to receive his visa, all the while working as a bricklayer. As planned, his Aunt Helen sponsored him with the U.S. government and sent him the money to purchase his ticket for his passage.

CHAPTER 11

<u>Coming to America</u>

1954 — Bremerhaven, West Germany — Dublin, Ireland —
Atlantic Ocean

At the end of August 1954, Helga stood on the dock in
Bremerhaven, kissing Helmut goodbye and promising him that she would sail for America as soon as he
could send for her. Helmut didn't look forward to the thought of
being alone in a new country and really wanted his girlfriend
with him when he landed in the U.S. Despite being alone, he was
excited when he boarded the 'SS Neptunia,' with Helga waving
goodbye from the dock. It was extremely hard to leave without
her, since he knew for certain that she was the woman he wanted
to marry. Her arrival in America wouldn't come soon enough for
him.

The ship was a thirty-five years old and had obviously
seen better days. It had exposed wooden beams below deck and

was so rickety, Helmut wondered if they would even make it across the Atlantic. Once they hit the English Channel and the boat rolled in the swell, Helmut succumbed to motion sickness. When the sea began to crash over the bow, he grew even more worried about the seaworthiness of their vessel. His cabin was small and on the ship's waterline so his port-light was more often than not, underwater. His cabin mates were two slightly older construction workers who already had jobs lined up in America, so the three men shared something in common.

The toilets and showers were down the hall and open to all men on that deck, but Helmut was more than a little shy about washing up in front of them. He usually waited until late at night to shower—when most of the men on their floor had gone to bed. He spent little time in his tiny cabin that felt quite claustrophobic and uncomfortable to him. He worried for much of the trip whether the Neptunia would be his ship of dreams taking him to the New World, or if it would simply expedite his passage to Davey Jones' Locker. He remembered the tragedy that had happened to the Titanic, a ship believed to be unsinkable. Helmut stayed on deck most of the first eight days until they had made it out to sea to calmer waters. There the ocean's more rhythmic motion improved both his nausea as well as much of his anxiety. Many of the other passengers were seasick and remained in their cabins throughout much of the journey, so he had above deck pretty much to himself most of the time.

The next week aboard the Neptunia was a time for serious introspection as Helmut made new friends aboard the ship. Many, like him, were searching for the same thing—a new life, but most importantly a free life to build a successful future. Helmut immediately gravitated to two attractive Irish girls around his age, Mandy and Bridgette, who were traveling together. Several other young men and women sort of formed a group with the three of them to talk and share their stories of their hopes and dreams in the land of 'Milk and Honey.' Despite the group's many struggles with different languages, they did their best to translate for each other as they spoke of what they knew of America and what they hoped to achieve there. Helmut had read as many books on America as he could find and he joined in their discussions about the Native American tribes and the original settlers. Helmut knew about Thanksgiving from his Aunt Helen and how America's harvest festival closely coincided with the German harvest festival of Erntedankfest, which had originated in Düsseldorf-Urdenbach. They also discussed the Revolutionary War and Civil War as well as America's participation in World War II. They all agreed that the Americans had been extremely helpful when they liberated Europe.

Helmut spent much of his time with Bridgette and Mandy since they were not only very attractive; they spoke English and did their best to help him to learn the language of his future homeland. The girls were both obviously attracted to Helmut— not only was he attractive—he had the ability to earn a good livelihood. In essence, he was a real catch, so both women flirted with him and he returned their affection in kind, but was never unfaithful to Helga. They managed to teach him many nouns and a few important phrases in English. Helmut knew quite a bit about English and Irish history and they spoke in his broken English about the girls' hometown of Dublin. They strolled the deck together during the day and Helmut would tease them and threaten to throw them overboard, so they would cling to him for dear life. He held hands with both of them and the three danced every night on deck to the ship's band. Bridgette and Mandy taught him to dance the cha cha and the rhumba and the three waltzed together under the stars. It was like a dream come true for Helmut and he couldn't help but wonder if America would be as magical as his trip to get there.

Helmut had his prize possession aboard with him—his guitar that he'd traded coffee and the ox for, but he didn't feel he was competent enough to play with the ship's musicians. He did however, join in the nightly parties singing and dancing with his friends since the band was there to entertain the immigrants.

Even though he could have all the alcohol he wanted, he didn't drink, but he did partake of as much soda as he wanted. To Helmut the food served aboard was fancier than he'd ever seen—it was a feast to him since he was used to a shortage of food in Germany. He was amazed at the generous smorgasbord with more roast beef, chicken, fish, vegetables, and fruits than he'd ever seen, as well as more cakes and puddings than he could even imagine.

Helmut felt as if he had the dinning room almost to himself on most days for breakfast, lunch, and dinner, due to the fact that many passengers stayed below deck because of their seasickness. Once his nausea had passed during the second week of the voyage he ate as much of the wonderful food as he could hold. One day the sailors aboard the ship caught a sea turtle while fishing and the chef made turtle soup, giving Helmut his first taste of turtle fresh from the sea.

It took a total of two weeks for the ship to arrive within sight of an enormous green woman wearing robes, bearing a torch above her crown of seven thorns. Lady Liberty was the first thing he saw of America as they approached land at dawn. As the ship entered the Port of New York he was able to see the giant statue from nearly every side. Helmut had no idea what he was looking at as the sun rose on the giant lady, but it excited him and somehow the sight of it gave him hope. Who was this woman lighting their way to the new world?

One of the young men in Helmut's group, Rienhardt, an educator from Germany, explained to Helmut that the massive copper statue had been a gift from France to the U.S. in 1886, intending to cement a friendship between the two countries. The Statue of Liberty as she was called, was the brainchild of, Édouard de Laboulaye, and the work of, Frederic Auguste Bartholdi, and commemorated the centennial anniversary of the signing of the Declaration of Independence. She stood tall in the harbor welcoming immigrants to Ellis Island as a beacon of 'freedom' to immigrants as they landed on American soil—represented by broken shackles at her feet.

Rienhardt chuckled, "That crown of thorns you mention is a symbol of her light, which shines across the world and the torch she carries stands for man's enlightenment, which lights the way to freedom and liberty." Rienhardt spoke English fluently and he recited the inscription at the base of the statue in English for Helmut: "Give me your tired, your poor, your huddled masses yearning to breathe free..." He then translated it into German for Helmut.

"Freedom and liberty," Helmut repeated in broken English. "I like the sound of that," he said smiling. Finally, he would have a chance to live his dream as a successful builder in America—to be valued for his work and talent while creating a new life far away from socialism, where the government controlled all means of production. Instead, it would mean holding the key to his own destiny. He knew that living in a true democracy would take some getting used to, but he looked forward to it. Although he'd had a small taste freedom in the newly developing democratic state of West Germany, he knew that conditions in America were even more favorable. He hoped to find success in the state of Wisconsin like his other family members, simply by dedication and hard work.

Helmut was lucky that the Neptunia made a successful journey: however a few years later a trip across the English Channel would send her to a watery grave. Luckily, all aboard were rescued by another ship, which was within sight of her when she ran aground and sank.

PART III

A DREAM OF A NEW LIFE

1954 – 2021 — New York — Wisconsin — Florida

United States of America

CHAPTER 12

Suspected as a Communist Spy

1954 — New York, New York — Milwaukee, Wisconsin

Once the Neptunia was docked, all passengers were allowed to disembark. All except Helmut, who waited impatiently for his turn to step onto American soil. Helmut, being an attractive young man of twenty, portrayed a respectable immigrant who had filled all of the requirements to enter the U.S.—a visa, a sponsor in Wisconsin, cash to live on for a while, and even a job arranged by his aunt and uncle. After several hours of waiting he was the last to be approached by the two immigration officers who were checking documents.

"Passport and visa," demanded the man in German, holding out his hand. Helmut smiled at the man in the brown suit and handed him his passport opened to his visa. The officer adjusted his glasses scrutinizing the passport, flipping pages to see where Helmut was born. When he saw that Helmut had been born in

East Prussia, not far from the Russian border, he closed the passport and suspiciously studied the hopeful young man who stood before him. "You are from East Prussia, Mr. Siewert."

"Yes...." answered Helmut uncertain if that was a question or a statement. "I was born in Ublick, but we escaped the Russians at the end of the war and went to live in Schraplau and then Domersleben."

"East Germany?" he stated flatly.

"Yes, but when I was seventeen, I crossed the boarder to live in the West so that I wasn't forced to join the Communist Party."

"How do we know you're not an agent sent by the Russians to America as a spy?" the immigration agent demanded.

Helmut laughed assuming the man was joking. It only took seconds to realize by the look on his face that he was perfectly serious. "But sir, I was issued a visa by the American consulate in Hamburg."

"Well it seems they made a mistake. We cannot allow you to leave this ship. You will have to return to Germany."

Helmut suddenly felt as if he'd been kicked squarely in the stomach. "Sir, I'm not going back to Germany. I have worked very hard to come to this country to join my family in

Wisconsin and have a chance to live totally free from Party control.   Please....I will jump off this ship and swim ashore if you don't let me off!"

Of course, Helmut neglected to disclose to the man that he didn't know how to swim. He tried his best to hide it, but inside, he was starting to panic at the thought of having all his dreams dashed by this man. Maybe he had been wrong about America. Maybe this country he'd dreamed of for so long was just as controlling as East Germany.

Helmut had heard about McCarthyism in America so he assumed that this was the anti-Communist system in action. Aunt Helen had written letters about a Wisconsin senator named Joseph McCarthy, who worked vigilantly to prevent communism from creeping into the U.S.—especially into his state. Helmut had used his aunt's address in Wisconsin on his immigration papers so he assumed that was what had triggered this interrogation. McCarthy's crackdown resulted in many indiscriminate accusations of subversion or treason by those in government, public office, Hollywood, academics, the media, as well as any organizations considered subversive, fascist, or totalitarian. No one it seemed was safe from being accused as a Communist. The senator aimed to prevent the seed of communism from seeping into the country, at all costs. Soviet spies were especially feared and the unassuming poor immigrant was the perfect plant in America for spreading the disintegration of democracy throughout the government. Helmut assumed that they thought he fit the perfect cover for a Communist spy. He wondered what his chances were of convincing them otherwise.

They held Helmut on the ship questioning him for three hours, until he had somewhat convinced them that he might in fact be simply a young man seeking a chance to find a better life. But, when they fingerprinted him there was hardly a trace of prints, which made them suspicious of this young man's motives all over again.

"Have you had your fingerprints burned off with acid?" the man asked.

"Excuse me, sir?" Helmut looked at his fingers, con-fused—uncertain what he meant.

"You have no fingerprints."

Helmut shrugged "I guess it's because I work with bricks and mortar everyday. Maybe they have been worn down. I don't know, sir, I've never been fingerprinted before."

Eventually, the officials released him into restricted cus-tody—meaning that they were not yet finished with him. Even though they allowed him to disembark the ship, they seized his documents and sent him to Sloan House in New York City, a YMCA-like boarding house.

He was not allowed to leave the immediate area and he had to report to the immigration offices on Fifty-third street every day at 10:00 a.m. sharp for further questioning—indefinitely. The offices were five miles away from the boarding house so he was forced to walk there and back each day, since the cost of a taxi would have quickly depleted his funds. Once there, the officials questioned him for more than two hours each time, repeating the same questions over and over trying their best to trip him up. Helmut however, was very clear and specific about his past, minus his arrest for trying to cross the border with his father and his answers were always consistent. It was when they asked about his participation in the Communist Youth FDJ/Freie Deutsche Jugend assembly outing in Berlin that he realized where their suspicions came from. He had never been initiated into the organization because his parents wouldn't allow him to join, nor did he want to become a member, but perhaps just his association with those children sent up a red flag.

"How many times did you travel to Berlin with the FDJ?" asked the same man in the brown suit from the ship."

"Only once," Helmut answered truthfully. "But I never joined….my parents were not Communists and they wouldn't allow me to join."

"Did you want to join?" he asked.

"No….I never wanted to join!" Helmut insisted.

"Where did you stay?"

"In a slaughter house."

"Excuse me?" The man took off his glasses and stared at Helmut, trying to intimidate him.

"It was an old concrete slaughterhouse they'd turned into a youth hostel. We slept on straw on a concrete floor."

"How long were you there?"

"Three days. The second day the American Army showed us films. Lucille Ball was in a trailer driving through the American highways in the mountains on vacation. It showed restaurants and open spaces," exclaimed Helmut. "It was like nothing I'd ever seen before. It was then that I decided I wanted to live in America."

"Do you expect me to believe that Lucille Ball of 'I Love Lucy' made you decide to immigrate to America?"

"What is I Love Lucy?"

The immigration man just looked at him, bewildered. "I'm going to have to have a talk with Desilu Productions."

Helmut suspected that his word on only participating in one FDJ assembly hadn't totally satisfied their concerns.

•

Helmut realized the funds that he'd sailed with would not last long in New York City, so he tried to find a way to call his aunt in Wisconsin. Of course, she wasn't aware that Immigration had detained him and she was very worried about him, since he hadn't arrived on his scheduled train. The problem was, Helmut didn't have a clue how to use a telephone. Thankfully, the manager of Sloan House was helpful in showing him how to place a collect call to his Aunt Helen. When he explained to her what had happened to detain him, she was very concerned about his precarious situation and promised to wire him more money to cover his stay in the city.

"Why would they think such a thing about you being a Communist spy, unless they have some reason to believe it?" Helen questioned him.

"I don't know, Aunt Helen, I left East Germany so I wouldn't be forced to join the Party."

"I understand that, my dear, but they don't. Just stick to your story and pray that they don't decide to send you home."

"But this is my home. I have no intention of returning to Germany no matter what."

Helen promised to send the money he needed via something called Western Union. She said he could find many offices around the city where he would be able to pick up his money by showing his passport. The only problem was that the immigration officers still held his passport. Luckily, one of the immigration officials took pity on Helmut and helped him retrieve his funds from a nearby Western Union office. He then had to quickly learn about U.S. money exchange of one mark to four U.S. dollars. He certainly didn't want to make a mistake and overpay for any purchases.

Once he had some additional cash, Helmut decided that since he was stuck in New York, he might as well see what the city had to offer. So, he began to play tourist instead of detained, immigrant refugee. The manager at the boarding house gave him directions to many sites and Helmut walked the city all day, everyday to see its many landmarks and to visit attractions such as Times Square and the Empire State Building, as well as seeing motion pictures for the first time. The skyscrapers in the city fascinated him and he hoped that he might build something that magnificent someday.   The tallest building he'd ever seen in Germany was only four stories.

On one of his treks around the city, Helmut met Paul, a slightly older European man who spoke German and was very helpful in him giving him information about the city. He invited Helmut to lunch and they discussed architecture and art, as well as the advantages of democracy. Helmut was impressed by his kindness, intelligence, and friendship and he joined him as his guest for lunch on a number of occasions. Paul even purchased tickets to Radio City Music Hall, so they could see a troop of dancers called the Rockettes.

Helmut was amazed by how rich the city was and how steeped in culture it felt, experiencing it all with Paul as his guide.   It was so vastly different was from anything he'd ever known in his sheltered life. He joined his friend a total of five times at restaurants that Helmut couldn't possibly afford, until it became very clear to him that his new friend, Paul, was interested in more than just his friendship. Helmut had never encountered a homosexual man before and he wasn't sure how to handle the situation. After all, Paul had been so generous to him. Once the light went on as to what this man was hoping for, or expecting, Helmut politely thanked him for his kindness and told him that he was not interested in any sort of personal relationship. He let Paul know that he was most certainly heterosexual and had a beautiful fiancé back in Germany, named Helga. Paul tried to change Helmut's mind by offering him housing, food, and a social life if he would only stay with him in New York, but Helmut politely declined the offer as graciously as he could. Paul was quite disappointed, but he understood and wished him luck with his resident status as well as his future marriage.

Helmut now had enough cash to take a taxi to and from the immigration office everyday, rather than walking the long distance for his daily interviews. After two weeks of their continual questioning, the officers decided to provisionally release him for a one-year probation period to live in Milwaukee with his aunt. They returned his passport and informed him that he was required to keep consistent employment and report to the Chicago immigration office at the end of the twelve-month period for his final review. He would then receive his resident status in the United States if he passed their investigation.

Helmut was so excited to be free to travel he quickly packed his meager belongings and went straight to the train station to purchase his ticket to Milwaukee. He was afraid that the immigration officials might change their minds, so he wanted to leave the city as quickly as possible. His trip to Milwaukee would require a transfer in Chicago to a different train station, in order to catch the train that would take him to the state of Wisconsin. So the minute he arrived in Chicago he found a taxi to take him to the next station. No one knew he was coming since he hadn't taken the time to call his aunt, but he assumed that finding her house would not be difficult since he had her address. When he finally arrived in Milwaukee he took a taxi from the train station to her home at Thirty-fourth and Hopkins. Helen and her husband, Herman, were surprised and relieved when he finally arrived. They had no children so they looked forward to his stay. Helmut couldn't believe that he'd finally reached his first home in America— a country built on Democracy, where he hoped to fulfill all his hopes and dreams.

CHAPTER 13

Building a New Life in a New World

1954 – 1958 — Milwaukee, Wisconsin

Helen and Herman Deblitz lived in a modest home in the suburbs of Milwaukee. Helmut's Aunt Helen worked as a hostess in a large, high-end hotel and his uncle, Herman, did marble fabrication for the Milwaukee Marble Company. Helen, Gustav's sister, who had been living in the U.S. since the early 1930s, had married Herman in Germany before they immigrated first to Canada and then to the U.S. They lived a simple, quiet life and never had any children. They did not own their own car, so Helmut bought a bus pass and rode all over the city the first few days he was there, hoping to learn his way around the city. He bought a map of Milwaukee and quickly got to know the area.

Thanks to his Uncle Herman, Helmut went to work with Heinz Stark, Herman's good friend, just five days after his arrival. Heinz was a contractor who had also emigrated from Germany, so Helmut was thrilled that he spoke German. Helmut's English was, at best, rudimentary, but he was good at pointing. Heinz had been an accountant in Berlin, but when he arrived in America, he bought a construction and masonry company, with little knowledge about the business of building. He had learned quickly, however and had astutely sponsored many German workers who were experts in the field in various trades. Helmut started his job with Stark as a helper, or mason-tender at $2.80 per hour and quickly learned the difference in tools and methods, as well as the American translations. Helmut excelled at his job so quickly that Stark promoted him to fulltime bricklayer within the first month. To Helmut's delight his new position included a nice raise in pay to $3.50 an hour.

Helmut worked hard to quickly learn the English language and took advantage of watching American television shows and listening to the radio with his aunt and uncle in the evenings. It not only helped him to understand English, but the radio programs, along with American newspapers and books taught him what really happened to the Jews in Europe during the war.

Helmut had heard rumors and, after the war, talked briefly with his father about the Jews when they were building their house in West Germany. But it wasn't until he got more detailed accounts about the camps that he truly understood the atrocities of Hitler and the Nazi regime. His aunt and uncle seemed to have known about the camps throughout much of the war since word had spread across America about the ethnic cleansing that was happening in Europe and the extermination of the Jews. It was hard for Helmut to believe the number of deaths in the camps, perpetrated by the Nazis. He discovered that over six million Jews, ten million Soviet citizens and POWs, almost two million Polish civilians, and a quarter-million disabled people died in the camps. Even more startling, these numbers did not include the thousands of criminals, political opponents, homosexuals, and those of other religious beliefs who also died in the camps.

The cleansing of the races was something Helmut found hard to accept and for the first time in his life he felt ashamed to tell people he was German. He especially felt guilty when dealing with Jewish clients who seemed to trust him implicitly with their business and their homes. How could they forgive any German people after what had happened to their families and loved ones? But surprisingly, they wanted to support him and work with him. Helmut was humbled to see that their character was strong enough to accept him and others like him into their community. In many ways, he got along better with the Jewish people than he did with German Christians. His Jewish friends counseled him, telling him that he was only a child and not to blame for the acts of those adults who blindly followed Hitler's rule. He felt lucky that America had even allowed the German people to immigrate to the United States after the war. He now understood why it had been so difficult for the American immigration officers to allow him to stay in this country.

At church, Helmut talked with other Germans about the atrocities in an attempt to learn how to deal with the guilt he felt at simply being German. Many of his congregation had also fled from the Russians and a number had been born in the Ukraine under Communist rule, so they understood both sides of the equation. He had been truly lucky—lucky that his father had held a position that allowed him to protect his family.

Helmut questioned his new Jewish friends about Hitler's reason for hating their people so intensely. They explained that Hitler was angry because their people were so successful and prosperous in business. Hitler came into power during the German recession and he blamed the Jewish people for their economic dilemma after reading the book, "The International Jew," a four-volume set of booklets originally published by a company owned by Henry Ford in the early 1920s. The publication blamed the Jews for everything evil in the world. Ironically, Hitler hadn't been aware until just before the war that his own paternal grandfather was Jewish—a fact that Hitler denied.

Helmut remembered how the Germans had destroyed the Jewish stores in Bischofswerder.   According to the Nazis the Jews ran the fashion, garment, fur, grocery, commerce, and textile industries in Germany before the war.   Starting with Kristallnacht, they destroyed all Jewish-run clothing and grocery stores. In the end, they also decimated the Jewish textile and garment industry and brought in German designers to create new, appropriately conservative fashions, which all Germans were forced to wear.   The exception was of course, the wives of generals who continued to don their Paris couture.   To Helmut's disbelief, some of his German friends still believed that the Jewish persecution was the Jews' own fault, and thought they shouldn't have controlled so many industries and the German economy. To Helmut's shock and dismay, they actually told him they felt the Jews were entirely to blame for what happened to them.

•.

Once Helmut's job was secure and he could sponsor Helga to come over, he wrote her asking her to finish her immigration paperwork as his fiancé, so they could be married as soon as possible in America. He needed a wife to help him build his new life. Besides, he was feeling extremely lonely spending all his nights with his aunt and uncle listening to the radio.   Helga used many reasons to stall applying to immigration and eventually wrote back nine months after he'd arrived to tell him she wanted to stay in Germany for two more years, so that she could finish her nursing apprenticeship. Hurt and frustrated, Helmut pushed her to leave right away, pointing out that she would just have to start over with different American requirements for her nursing career. He wrote her of the wonderful things in America, but no matter how much he tried to make her understand how important it was for her to be with him, she refused to leave until she had finished her schooling. But the truth be told, Helmut finally realized that Helga was simply not ready to leave the security of her parents home, which made him feel as if she did not fully trust him to protect and provide for her. This realization truly hurt Helmut's ego and he took her decision as a sign of rejection.

In the meantime, Helmut had met another young, German girl with the same name and birthday as his fiancé in Germany. Helmut and Helga Treu both attended the German Bethel Baptist Church, where they met. She was not nearly as attractive as his Helga in Germany, but she had beautiful legs. After writing Helga in Germany trying to convince her to come, Helmut gave up and wrote her telling her he'd found someone else to marry, unless she changed her mind about coming to America. She was terribly distraught since she thought he was in love with her and would surely wait for her as long as necessary. But Helmut was wrought with an impatience that he would live to regret and he broke off his engagement in Germany.

•

Before he knew it, it was time for Helmut to go back to Chicago for his final immigration review, since his one-year probationary period was ending. He was excited about obtaining his permanent residency in the U.S., yet nervous that they would find a reason to deny him residency. On the anniversary of his first year in America he rented a car for his drive to Chicago and met with his assigned immigration officer. Based on his employer's recommendation, he was cleared and granted permanent residency in the U.S., with a pathway to citizenship. Helmut was thrilled. He had finally reached his dream and was on the way to becoming an American citizen.

Feeling secure now to invest in his future in America, Helmut immediately bought a lot in Butler, a small town in southeastern Wisconsin. He paid twelve hundred dollars cash for the property, from his savings over the last year, and also purchased a used car for three hundred dollars. Finally, he felt comfortable investing in his future with the new Helga in America.

Helmut and Helga Treu went to many church-sponsored outings together. They were both members of the church's youth group and worked together on events for the congregation's children. They went swimming in the cold waters of Lake Michigan and she taught him how to swim. They often went to movies and one night Helga skipped her father's choir practice to go on a date with Helmut. Her father, who was in charge of the choir, was so furious that he hit her hard across her face, knocking her down, in front of Helmut. It was at that moment, that Helmut decided he had to get her away from her father's control and his violent temper.

Helmut and Helga Treu dated for a year and three months before they married. He wanted to earn enough money so they could build their own house. Helga worked on the assembly line in Milwaukee for Briggs and Stratton, a tractor and lawnmower manufacturing company. She made a decent salary for a woman, so she also saved money for their new home. Helmut's aunt and uncle always refused to accept rent from him and Helen even made him sandwiches for lunch every day. Thanks to their many kindnesses, he was able to save most of his salary. The only extravagance in his life was when he and Helga went to the movies together. Helmut felt that marrying Helga would be a good business decision and he believed that she would make a good mother for their children. Their marriage was planned; however, a few days before the wedding, his aunt asked Helmut if they could talk privately.

"Helmut, I'm a little concerned about your marriage to Helga," Helen said in a very serious tone.

"Why is that Aunt Helen? She's a very nice girl and I believe she loves me."

"Yes, I know she does, dear....it's her family that concerns me."

"But why is that?"

"Well, she's not from the best upbringing and how a girl is raised puts great bearing on who she is and how she will raise her own family," Helen explained tactfully. "You know I'm sixty-five and I'm retiring soon and we would love for you to stay with us until your other Helga could come over. I know how much you love her."

"Aunt Helen, I appreciate your concern, but I can't wait that long for a wife. I want to start my family now, not two years from now. Besides, I think you are judging her unfairly. Just because she has a terrible father and older brother it doesn't mean that she will treat her own children that way."

Helen thought for a minute and nodded, realizing that Helmut's mind was made up. The last thing she wanted was to drive a wedge between herself and her nephew, whom she loved as if he was her own son.

"Well then my dear....I wish you and Helga all the best."

Helmut gave Helen a hug "Thank you for looking out for me, but I know what I'm doing."

That little talk with his aunt caused Helmut some serious introspection. He knew he was definitely infatuated with Helga, but he wasn't really sure that he was in love with her. Certainly not the way he had loved his Helga in Germany. A few days later, as he stood at the front of the church on their wedding day, waiting for her to walk down the aisle, he debated if he should just walk out due to his doubts. He suddenly realized that he'd made a huge mistake by refusing to wait for the love of his life to come from Germany. They had been so good together. She was easygoing, unlike his high-strung wife-to-be and he worried how things might escalate down the road. His impatience had cost him a great deal and he realized that he had simply settled for a quick solution to his loneliness. If only she'd come to America when he asked. As much as he loved them, he was bored with living with his aunt and uncle, staying home and listening to the radio every night. He was lonely and felt as if he needed a life partner—someone to support him in his future successes and to love him despite any failures.

It was a time when it would have been totally inappropriate to live with a woman without being married. His decision to marry Helga Treu had been a practical one and Helmut was a practical man. That might be a good attribute in business, but was practicality the right basis for a marriage? No matter, he was a man of his word and as his bride walked down the aisle, he knew it was far too late to change his mind. They were married on December 3, 1955 in Milwaukee's German Zion Baptist Church and the newlyweds spent their honeymoon at the Iron Mountain Ski Resort & Lodge in Michigan's Upper Peninsula.

Helmut had skied only once, at eight years old on home-made skis cut out of drums, but he was a quick learner and enjoyed spending the days on the mountain. Helga however, refused to ski and the honeymoon was far from idyllic for her. She hated the cold and snow and didn't find it to be a very romantic setting for their honeymoon. She spent most of their three-day trip in the lodge waiting for Helmut. Maybe it wasn't the most romantic honeymoon they could have chosen, but he really enjoyed learning to ski and he wasn't really into 'romance' anyway. When they returned to Milwaukee they lived with her parents for a while, since bricklayers couldn't work in sub-zero weather and they needed to save their money to start building their new home. This was even less romantic, since living with Helga's father was no picnic.

As the frigid weather eased, Helmut worked in the evenings at the factory for The Milwaukee Electric Tool Company, which allowed him work on building their house during the day. He quickly became a valued and well-paid employee of the tool company, since he was especially good at metric conversion. The company had recently converted the entire factory to the metric system and most of the employees had not yet gotten the hang of the new conversion system.

•

In late December 1955, two years after Stalin's death, the Siewert family got word that Lydia's brother, August Fester, had been released from the Siberian POW camp where he had been imprisoned in 1945.   Helmut kept up with the news from Germany and he was thrilled to know that his uncle was alive and finally a free man. He learned that the West German Chancellor, Konrad Adenauer, flew to Moscow to meet with Russian Premiere Nikita Khrushchev, and insisted that before diplomatic relations could be established, the Siberian prisoners would have to be freed. Konrad paid for the release of the POWs and recovered twenty thousand men and women. However, only five thousand would live long enough to see their new homes in Germany.

August returned to Bochum, West Germany, where food and living quarters were provided for him. He managed to locate his wife, Emma and daughter, Edith, in Gramten, Poland, which was still occupied. He did his best to get his wife and daughter to join him, but they were afraid. Both women had psychiatric issues resulting from being molested by the Russians. When they did eventually move back to Germany the daughter was placed in an institution and his wife was treated for her psychiatric disorder. By then, August was involved with another woman, however he did have his wife come to live with them.

•

On his own time, Helmut designed a typical German brick house with an A-frame roof with dormer windows to give it charm, as well as a large balcony. He built it from twenty-two-foot long rafters to give it strength, which he managed to install all by himself. The house consisted of a basement and two rooms on the main level. He built a full bathroom upstairs and a half bath downstairs—a luxury after having no indoor plumbing for most of his early life. Once the house was finished, he poured a concrete driveway for their new car and planted some juniper trees in the yard.

Except for the plumbing and heating, Helmut did all the work on the house himself in only six months. He was quite proud of his first attempt at building and it served as a very comfortable little cottage for him and Helga. Shortly after the house was finished, he decided to start his own masonry company. When he gave notice at Milwaukee Electric, they begged him to stay and offered him a much higher salary, but Helmut was determined to strike out on his own and he took the risk, certain that he could achieve whatever he set out to do. After all, he had out-run the Russian Army at the age of ten and that little boy had turned into a very confident, independent, and capable man.

It wasn't long before Helga became pregnant and Helmut realized that their tiny house in Butler would soon be too small, so he traded it for a duplex on Capital Drive in Milwaukee. The second unit came with a tenant and Helmut found the rental to be a great help. Already his trade in homes was turning out to be a lucrative one. Their first child, Michael Jon, was born on April 15, 1957 and Helga quickly became pregnant with their second son, Thomas Scott, born fourteen months later. Luckily, Helga's mother babysat their children at her home, while they both worked. The insurance from Helga's job went a long way where the hospital bills were concerned. Helga however, didn't seem to be adjusting well to motherhood. She was eventually diagnosed with hysteria and depression and her mood swings became more and more severe. Helga no longer wanted to take care of the children, or the house, so her mother and Helmut had to do every-thing. Years later they would re-diagnose Helga's mental health issue as a bi-polar disorder

•

Helmut was starting to get more work than he could han-dle, with his issues at home, and he started thinking about his cousin, Wilfried, who was an accountant. He had approached Helmut before the wedding suggesting that they start a construction company together, along with a friend from church, Siegfried Herman, a concrete finisher. Helmut was friends with Siegfried and had even dated his sister, Erica, for a short period before he met Helga, but he had decided that she was too far too young for him. He had however, managed to stay friends with Siegfried after the breakup. Uncle Herman tried to convince Helmut not to go into business with Siegfried, since he didn't feel he was a hard enough worker, but Wilfried vouched for him and Helmut trusted Wilfried implicitly. The two had been through the worst together when they were on the wagon train, so Helmut went along with his cousin's advice. Helmut and Wilfried moved forward in organizing the company, but unfortunately, Wilfried was suddenly drafted into the U.S. Army for basic training, leaving Helmut and Siegfried to run the business. A decision was made that Siegfried would buy Wilfried out and they named the new company Herman and Siewert.

For six months business slowed, forcing Helmut to pick up extra work back at the Milwaukee Electric Tool Company, but eventually more jobs came in and they grew very busy. Helmut quickly realized that his uncle was right—Siegfried was not the most astute businessman, or the fastest worker, so he insisted that they dissolve their partnership. From that point forward, Helmut simply subcontracted the cement work out to Siegfried. This made him see that subcontracting work for all other trades, from experienced craftsmen, was the most profitable way for a small company to do business.

After a year, Helmut had more business than he could handle alone. Luckily, about that time his wife's brother, Willie Treu, was discharged from the army and went to work for Helmut running sales for the construction business. After two years they had more jobs than they could handle and needed thirty full-time employees to keep up with the work. This is when Helmut decided to follow Heinz Stark's example and sponsor several masons from Germany to come and work for him. He also realized how well he and Willie worked together and he made him a forty-five percent partner in the company.

•

Once word got out about the horror of the Holocaust and the POW camps still operating in East Germany, many German and Jewish charities sprang up throughout the U.S., especially in Wisconsin due to the large German and Jewish population. Helmut and his aunt Helen were big supporters and Helmut was moved by the loyalty his business received from their many Jewish clients. Mr. Busselberg, who printed Helmut's business cards, was kind enough to give the cards to all of his Jewish clients.

From these contacts, Helmut built nearly one thousand founda-
tions and basements for twenty-four-foot by thirty-foot ranch-
style houses, with more than half of his clientele being Jewish.
Numerous other clients and developers, such as Sidney Freeman,
Ellen Crawford, and the Wasserman Brothers came to Helmut to
either hire him or partner with him.

•

Helmut kept his word and continued to send money back
home to his family in West Germany. Marlene, who had turned
sixteen and still lived at home with Gustav and Lydia, got a job as
a baker's apprentice in the Bremen Bakery. Bremen was near the
coast and approximately eight miles from home, so the bakery
provided living quarters for the girls. She made so little money it
hardly made a difference with the family finances; however, she
was provided food. She helped prepare the orders for bread,
cakes, cookies, rolls and other baked goods, starting at 4 a.m. By
6 a.m. Marlene, along with ten to twelve other girls, delivered the
yummy, warm treats to customers' homes all over town. One day,
Helmut received a telegram informing him that Marlene was hit
by a car while making her morning deliveries in the dark. She
suffered a severe concussion and spent several weeks in the hospital. Delivering hot cross buns in the dark was not the safest
choice of employment, so after she recovered, she went to work
for a local grocer.

CHAPTER 14

Fires at Work – Fires at Home

1958 – 1962 — Milwaukee, Wisconsin

In 1958 Helmut made his first trip back to West Germany to visit his family. He felt that taking Helga on vacation might be just what she needed. When they arrived at his parents' home, Helga took an immediate disliking to Lydia, when she spotted a framed picture on the wall of Helmut with the other Helga. The Siewerts had not made it to their wedding so they had never met their daughter-in-law, and they were not aware of her severe mood swings. They did their best to welcome her to their home; however, Helga shocked them all when she removed the picture from the wall and cut the first Helga clean out of the photo, before re-hanging it in the same spot. Lydia was livid, but with the hope of keeping peace in the family she held her tongue. In the end it did no good since it all seemed to go downhill from there.

Between Helga's icy demeanor and the chilly temperature, their first night in Germany was extremely cold. The un-
insulated masonry walls were no help since they kept in no
warmth so Helmut stoked the wood stove up as high as he could
in a desperate effort to stop Helga's unending complaints about
freezing to death. When he bent over to pick up more kindling for
the fire his pajamas caught on fire as he backed up to the stove,
badly burning his buttock. Helmut dashed to the water-filled
hand-basin to put the fire out. It seemed his tuchus was in very
hot water in more ways than one.

Helmut's second mistake, outside of bringing Helga home
in the first place, was to take Lydia out to a restaurant as a treat,
since she had never eaten out before. Lydia cried through most of
the meal because she thought Helga disliked her cooking.

"Mutti, we simply wanted to treat you to dinner so you
didn't have to work so hard while we were here."

"That's okay Helmut, I understand that you no longer like
my cooking," Lydia sniffled.

"That's not it at all," Helmut exclaimed trying to reason
with her. "We eat out all the time in America, that's very usual
there."

"Oh I see, you mean that women in America don't know how to cook," Lydia said, glaring directly at Helga with a new understanding.

Helmut swallowed hard as he watched the five-alarm fire start to blaze in Helga's eyes. He knew he was in for a very long week on their German vacation, since no matter what he did; Helmut always seemed to find himself in the hot seat.

•

Back in Wisconsin, Helmut's business continued to expand, thanks to a Jewish investor, Maurice Steiner, who talked Helmut into building his first twenty-four-family complex in Kenosha, Wisconsin. Helmut set up a partnership with Steiner, even though he was nervous about taking on such a large project for their own development, but they managed to complete the building within five months and kept it as a profitable rental for nearly five years.

After that Helmut and Maurice bought more land on the same street and then built a twenty-family building. Having learned from the first building, they built the second in record time. They were in the finishing stages of construction when they hired Mark Ruffalo *(the actor's father)* as a construction painter, to spray lacquer on the doors of the building. Unfortunately, he left his cleaning rags in a covered bucket and they ignited in the summer heat, burning the new building right to the ground. Luckily, Helmut had insurance to cover his losses, however, the insurance company wanted to hire a different contractor from Kenosha to do the rebuild. Helmut objected and insisted that if another contractor were to be hired to rebuild and finish his project, their company would have to buy him out. Finally, the other contractor agreed to the deal and Helmut walked away with an acceptable profit.

•

Two years after the project fire, Helmut's company was building a sixty-four-unit structure for another developer. It was the dead of a very cold winter and the mortar from the day before would freeze overnight. This made it necessary for the masons working on the project to use a torch to thaw out the frozen mortar. One very cold afternoon, the masons held their torches to one spot for too long, not realizing that the wood behind the mortar had started to smolder. During the night it caught the building on fire, burning it to the ground. After a three-month court case with, John Brady, Helmut's long-time attorney defending them, the judge determined that, Danny, the head mason on the job, held the torch too long against the mortar and the two-by-four and the fiber for insulation behind smoldered overnight and caught the building on fire. Henceforth, Danny took on the moniker of 'Danny the Torch.'

•

Helmut began a new and much larger project from the proceeds of that settlement—sixty-two side-by-side townhomes on the same street. With so many new units to sell Helmut realized how necessary it was to increase his sales department, so in addition to Willie Treu, he hired another salesman named Russ Morton. Russ was excellent at sales, but he lacked a broker's license. Helmut insisted that he obtain one so that they could handle all their sales in-house, rather than go through an outside agent. Helmut made the decision to sell the twenty-four-family, two-bedroom building to another company and he set a price, tasking Russ with his first assignment to sell all the units.

Two days later, instead of selling their twenty-four-unit building, Russ signed a contract to buy another company's three-story, thirty-unit efficiency apartment building. Helmut pointed out that he had no authority to sign on his behalf to purchase this property, however Russ insisted that he couldn't cancel the contract. Helmut's attorney, John Brady, negotiated a quit-claim deed to erase the transaction; however, the sellers had already put a fictitious mortgage on the building in Helmut's name. Helmut went to court and won, but it took a month and a half to settle the dispute, before it was finally thrown out—the judge determining that the seller never had a legal contract on the deal. In the meantime, Helmut collected the rent on all the units for that month and a half to cover the legal costs. At the end of the fiasco, Helmut fired Russ who wept like a baby. Helmut finally sold the original building that had cost him two hundred five thousand dollars for two hundred forty thousand, turning his first major profit. This thrilled Helmut since a thirty-five thousand dollar profit in 1960 was a lot of money.

•

Helmut's business was growing in leaps and bounds, as were his children, who saw little of their busy father. It seemed that while he was busy putting out literal fires a work, new ones were always smoldering at home due to Helga's state of mind. The size of their family was also growing fast in number, since in 1960 Helga discovered she was pregnant again and another son, Jeffrey Helmut, was born. As far as Helmut was concerned, that was enough children, but Helga desperately wanted a baby girl and was determined to keep trying for another child.

Helmut loved his family; however, his early years of poverty and strife had instilled in him a stalwart work ethic, not to mention a strong sense of fear of never wanting to be in a position of need again. Helga resented the fact that Helmut was gone all the time and that he spent very little time with her and the children. In turn, Helmut was frustrated that Helga took little, or no, interest in his business affairs since he would have loved her help and support in his success.   He often thought of what life would have been like had he been patient enough to wait for his previous fiancé, Helga, to come from Germany.   Helmut knew he was lucky not only to have survived the war, but to have also had the opportunity to create a good life in America.   He had few regrets, but not waiting for Helga weighed heavily on him as one of the worst decisions he'd ever made.   He had proved to be a shrewd businessman, but regarding his mastery of love and marriage, he was lacking equal acumen.   In truth he was sad that he had lost the only true love he had ever felt and was frustrated by his wife's lack of respect and support for what he'd achieved.

In 1960, Helmut's Aunt Helen, Gustav's sister, sponsored Helmut's father to move to the U.S. by ocean liner. Lydia stayed behind in their home in West Germany because Dieter was still in school and the fact that she suffered from terrible motion sickness.   Lydia wanted her husband to assess the situation in America before they made the major commitment to sell their home and move. She also wanted Dieter to finish school and his apprenticeship as an electrician.   When Gustav arrived, he was quite overweight and Helen put him on a strict diet, in an attempt to slim him down for his own health.   After two months, Gustav could stand it no longer and he called Helmut, demanding that his son pick him up because Helen was starving him to death.   Helmut picked Gustav up and took him directly to the nearest steakhouse.

After two orders of the largest sirloin steaks they had, Gustav was starting to feel his old self again.

"Listen dad, I would love to have you stay with us, but you know how difficult Helga can be. I think you're much better off staying with Aunt Helen."

"No, no….my sister's trying to starve me to death."

"She's simply trying to help you get healthier. You're overweight dad."

"Overweight, nonsense. I may as well be back in that prisoner-of-war camp. I think I ate better food there than the salads, fruit, and vegetables my sister forces me to eat, ugh! I miss my sausage and bologna."

"She's not trying to starve you, she loves you and wants to take care of you. Don't worry, I'll take you out for dinner more often so you can eat more meat."

"I think it's time to go home to your mother, Helmut. Book me the next flight to Germany."

"But I thought you were afraid to fly."

"I'm more afraid of starving to death."

So that was that and within forty-eight hours, Gustav was on his way back to Germany.

•

Helmut and Willie found a new piece of land for their next building project in Rockford, Illinois. They formed an ambitious plan to build one hundred sixty-four one, two, and three bedroom townhouses, but they needed financing. Helmut had a connection with a mortgage company, Metropolitan Life, who quickly agreed to give them a loan to buy the land, build, and rezone the property from agricultural to multi-family dwellings. The largest project of his career, so far, went successfully and their company kept the property for the next five years, renting the units for a nice profit.

•

In 1962 Helga was thrilled when she gave birth to a baby girl they named, Janet Marie. By now, Helmut had started drinking with his architect buddies and business associates over many extended lunches. His hour-and-a-half lunches soon turned into three hours and one Brandy Manhattan turned into three or four drinks. Things were not going well at home and it seemed that with each successful project, as well as with each new child, Helga's mental state deteriorated into more paranoia and intensified fits of anger. By the time Janet was born, not even the baby girl she had dreamed of for so long seemed to satisfy Helga's anxiety. She wanted Helmut at home to spend more time with her and the kids. Trying to appease her, Helmut built her a beautiful two-story, four-bedroom home fifteen miles away in Brookfield, Wisconsin and moved the family there. The new brick home had a two-car garage, a swimming pool, and a fenced-in yard for the children. Helmut was very proud of the fact that he'd managed to build it for only thirty-two thousand dollars. Helga had quit working by this point and Helmut felt it necessary to work even harder to ensure he could provide his family—something he'd only dreamed of as a child.

Helmut's construction office was in Rockford, Illinois and he was in charge of all of the projects on their slate, as well as of their eighteen-truck yard for the masonry company in Brookfield, Wisconsin. He found it necessary to drive there twice a week, but the two-hour trip quickly became a burden, so Helmut and Willie decided to buy a plane to use for the business. For a few weeks both Helmut and Willie had been taking flying lessons— inspired by a business associate, David Fuegel, who owned his own plane. Helmut had received his pilot's license quickly and Willie was about to test for his, so it was the perfect time to invest in an airplane. Cutting down his travel time would free up a great deal of time in Helmut's schedule allowing him to spend more time at home with the family. The new arrangement worked out quite well for them, as they took turns flying back and forth to their jobsites in their own plane. For long-distance flights the two would still use commercial airlines, but they would use their plane for their vacations to Florida and other parts of the east coast.

David Fuegel, proposed that Helmut go into business with him on public-turnkey housing throughout the Midwest. Helmut was skeptical, since he didn't really understand the concept of low-income public housing, or turnkey housing until David picked him up in Milwaukee and they flew to Illinois to look at projects and property. Together, they bought building sites in Illinois and Wisconsin and their architects designed the new projects. They then presented their proposals for nineteen four-family and two-family units to the local housing boards as well as to the United States Department of Housing and Urban Development (HUD)—an agency that provided financing for public housing. In 1964, HUD approved their first project near the Fairgrounds Park Development in Rockford, Illinois. The tenant was required to pay the maintenance and upkeep fees for four years and then their company would be eligible to buy the units from HUD. They would then be free to convert them into profitable condominiums.

After they successfully built the Fairgrounds project, HUD then required them to build scattered housing units throughout the city of Rockford. Helmut's company would buy the land, design and draw the plans, propose the specs and locations, and submit them to the HUD office in Chicago, which would take two months to review.   During his trip to Chicago, Helmut looked back on his very first trip to the Windy City when he received his final immigration determination.   Back then he was uncertain if he'd even be allowed to stay in America.   He suddenly realized how far he'd come in just nine' years time and he felt very grateful for his success.

Helmut and David Fuegel built two more successful projects together. Helmut ritually attended his three-hour lunches with the same architects and associates until he finally came to realize that Helga's worsening psychiatric problems at home were partially a result of his neglect. He then realized he would have to change his bad habits if he wanted to improve the situation at home. Helga had started sleeping all day and was totally unable to take care of the children at that point. Thankfully, her mother stepped in to watch the children and keep a close eye on Helga. Her hysteria and depression were quickly worsening and Helmut and Helga's mother realized that hospitalization was her only hope, considering her condition. Helga was committed for psychiatric care and Helmut's mother-in-law moved into the house to help Helmut with the children.

·

Later that year, Helmut set up a sponsorship for his sister, Marlene, to immigrate to the U.S. as well as his father's youngest brother, Uncle Otto. He loved Otto's sense of humor and he became one of Helmut's closest friends, even though he was twenty years older than Helmut. During the war, Otto had been a sergeant in the German military police. Near the end of the war, Otto had been captured by the American Army in Italy and had driven a truck for them until he left to move to the U.S. When he arrived in America, Helmut immediately put him to work driving trucks for his business. Otto quickly became engaged to a German woman, whom he met after he arrived, named Iris Vogel. Very shortly after their engagement she developed an acute case of pneumonia and passed away. Otto promptly married her younger sister, Ester.

Later that year when Helmut's sister, Marlene, moved to the U.S., she stayed in his home for the first four months. Helga, who was now back home, quickly grew to dislike her sister-in-law and she insisted that Helmut find Marlene more suitable quarters. So, Helmut helped Marlene find a housekeeping job for a wealthy homeowner on the lakefront, where she could live and work. Soon she met a man named Richard Zucknik and became seriously involved with him and it wasn't long before she found herself pregnant. They had a quick cover-up marriage, which caused Helga, who was a staunch Christian, to dislike her that much more. This of course drove a further rift between Helmut's wife and his family.

Later in Germany in 1962, Dieter was nearly finished with his apprenticeship as an electrician, so Helmut brought his parents to the U.S. by ship for a vacation. They were amazed by America's affluence and the fact that it was so much larger than they had ever imagined. Finally, Helmut convinced his mother, with the help of several Valium, to fly in his plane to his condos in North Palm Beach, Florida. Both Gustav and Lydia were overwhelmed by the Atlantic Ocean and they quickly fell in love with the warmth and beauty of Florida. Having overcome their fear of flying, they returned to Germany by plane after a few weeks.

CHAPTER 15

A Self-Made Man

1962 – 1975 — Palm Beach, Florida — Milwaukee, Wisconsin

Helmut was starting a new project in Palm Beach, Florida, which took him from home for longer periods of time. These long absences made Helga spiral even further into her dark, depressive moods, which would often swing to hysterical tirades.   During those years she required multiple psychiatric commitments, especially when Helmut was away on business. She was convinced that her husband's business trips consisted of romantic liaisons with numerous beautiful consorts and nothing Helmut said could convince her otherwise.

Occasionally while he was gone, Helga would be able to look after the kids, but most of the time his mother-in-law, Magdalena Treu would watch them when he couldn't.   Helga often confronted Helmut about the imaginary affairs, but Helmut had always pooh-poohed her accusations as more of her paranoid delusions, causing her to fall even further into her quickly deepening rabbit hole.

Up until that point Helga's delusions had been a figment of her imagination, however, when he started on his second forty-two-unit project in Fort Lauderdale, Florida on Cordova Dr., he met and hired a woman named, Madelyne Rizzoli to work for him in his Rockford, Illinois office. Before long Helmut gave into temptation and began an affair with this beautiful, sensitive, and caring woman. He found himself renting a furnished apartment and moving in with her, as well as flying her down with him to the new Fort Lauderdale project. He sought comfort in the relationship, which helped to assuage his emotional loneliness.

Helmut started keeping three sets of clothes split between his home with Helga, the apartment with Madelyne, and his Palm Beach condo. He was living a duplicitous life and he found it hard to fully justify his reasons for creating it. His affair with Madelyne lasted for three months including nearly four weeks on one of the trips to his Palm Beach condo. While there they would drive down to Miami to dine, many evenings, with his friends.

Upon his return home from his month-long rendezvous with Madelyne, Helga confronted him by flying into a rage, once again accusing him of having an affair. During a weak moment, Helmut threw up his hands in frustration confessing to her that he had indeed been with another woman during his so-called 'business trip.' Having her worst fears confirmed, Helga went absolutely crazy at the news that she had so strongly suspected. She quickly spiraled into a total nervous breakdown and once again required hospitalization. Rather than move out, Helmut decided it was imperative that he remain in his home with his children, since he realized Helga was totally unable to care for them. He was grateful that Magdalena, his mother-in-law, stayed with him to help with the kids. She was sympathetic to his indiscretions realizing how difficult his marriage to Helga had been and she understood how he might be temped to stray from her daughter's bed, considering her condition. Helmut immediately broke off the relationship with Madelyne and helped her financially to move to Florida. He told her that he regretted the turn of events, but he could have no more contact with her in the future for the sake of his children. Madelyne cared a great deal for Helmut and was deeply saddened by his decision, since they both knew how compatible and happy they had been together.

•

Helmut's newest thirty-six-unit, one and two-bedroom condo development in Palm Beach demanded a great deal of his time in Florida, but luckily he had a reliable sub-contractor named Jack Knippel who handled most of the physical construction. Helmut decided it would be best to keep one of the two-bedroom units on the Intracoastal Waterway for his own use, since he was required to spend so much time there overseeing the project. He also purchased an eighteen-foot fishing boat, which he knew he could write off as an entertainment expense for his associates.

While Helga's mental status was continuing to spiral further downward back in Wisconsin, Helmut realized that due his own bad habits he had tumbled into a deep vortex. He knew he would quickly have to curb his addictions before he found himself so deep in his smoking and alcohol abuse it would be impossible to clean up his life. Rather than go to a rehab center, Helmut made a decision. If he had been able to escape the Russian Army at ten years old, he knew he could break a few bad habits on his own without an intervention. He took one week off of work and went offshore alone everyday into the Gulf Stream on his fishing boat with no food, cigarettes, or alcohol—only water to drink. He had read Hemmingway's, *The Old Man and the Sea,* a book about the struggle between man and nature and he saw himself in Hemingway's character, Santiago. But, instead of battling a giant marlin out in the Gulf Stream, much like Hemingway himself, he was battling giant demons of his own nature that he'd never had the guts to face before. For seven days he stayed on the sea alone, burned by the sun—eating only at night when he returned home to his condo on the Intracoastal. He dealt, for the first time, with all that he had refused to acknowledge before–

–all he'd seen in Germany at the end of the war; the little girl swept away by the icy river; those refugees on the wagon train blown apart behind them while trying to escape ahead of the Russian Army; his little Jewish friend's ultimate demise in the concentration camp; the love he'd lost when Helga refused to leave Germany to come to America to be his wife; his guilt of how those of his homeland had committed genocide against the Jewish people; his shortfalls as a husband and father; as well as his infidelities. He had been mistaken that his most important job in life was to be successful—to make money to provide an upper-class home for his family. So, he vowed that he would do better. He would find a way to spend more time with his family and he would do what he could to help the Jewish community to recover from the horrors of the war. They had been loyal to him as clients and partners and even though he was German, they self-lessly accepted that he was not personally responsible for their people's hardships.

At the end of the week Helmut had quit the cigarettes and alcohol. He had already broken off his relationship with Made-lyne—now he just had to avoid any future extra-marital relation-ships. He had to find another way to assuage his loneliness and provide himself comfort without any of his previous vices.

•

The Fort Lauderdale project was built as a rental property, but Helmut and his partner, Sidney Friedman the heir to his family's department stores, Schuster's and Gimbels in Milwaukee, decided midway to convert the units into condos. It took nine months to build and three months prior to completion, the condos were sold out. Friedman was a strange man who kept his yacht docked behind his house in Fort Lauderdale and would traverse the Intracoastal Waterway north to Lake Michigan and the St. Lawrence Seaway on his yacht. He was involved with a number of insurance companies and his office was only three blocks from his home in Florida. He would walk to work everyday in shorts and flip-flops enjoying his carefree lifestyle. He invested in Helmut's newest project and they received their construction financing from First Wisconsin National Bank. He was so impressed with Helmut's success that he also invested in three additional two-story buildings in North Palm Beach and designed to be rental units and condos.

•

While Helmut still owned the Fort Lauderdale project, he brought his parents from Germany for a another visit to Florida. Between the warm weather and delicious, plentiful food, they were in heaven. Lydia began to look forward to the treat of dining out in America, since for the first time in her life she didn't have to cook. Helmut took them to a restaurant, which bragged that their pork shanks were so large, if you finished one, you would get a second for free. Gustav nearly died eating two, but he actually managed to polish off both of them. By the time he ate the last bite, he was gasping for air from gorging himself.

It wasn't long after this that Helmut's Aunt Helen fell sick and was diagnosed with cancer. Within eight weeks she had succumbed to the disease—Helmut was devastated by her passing. She and her husband had given the Siewert family the chance to build a better life in America. The childless couple had sponsored almost every family member who had found their way to a new life in this new, prosperous country. To Helmut, she had become like a second mother to him.

•

When Dieter was eighteen, Helmut received a letter from his younger brother that he had married a woman, also named Helga, and they were living with his parents. Dieter and Gustav had taken a loan and bought a second lot, next to the one Helmut had originally purchased. The two were in the process of building a larger, two-story house, while converting the original house to a garage. It was Dieter's plan to move into the upstairs above Gustav and Lydia, with his new wife. Dieter had become successful selling household appliances and was doing well working as an electrician. He was bringing in a decent income for the family, so Helmut felt that his parents were in good hands with his younger brother. But he still couldn't wait for the time that he would be able to sponsor his entire family to come to America.

·

Helmut and his partner Willie Treu were building a nine-story project for the elderly back in Dixon, Illinois for the Housing Authority. It was not long after Helga had been committed once again to a psychiatric facility, that one of the partners had to fly to the site to check on its progress. It was Helmut's turn to go, but due to his situation at home, Willie took his place to fly to Illinois. The day he left the terrible news came—Willie had been killed in a crash during takeoff in their plane. Willie had always had a bad habit of checking the gauges as he was taxiing and he didn't always look up to check for other planes on the unmanned runway. Helmut had warned him several times about this, but that day he cross-collided at a runway intersection when a student pilot landed ahead of him coming in from a different direction. It appeared that Willie had forgotten to turn on the radio and while the plane's nose was up for takeoff, he couldn't see the crossing plane. The two planes collided causing an explosion, burning both planes and their pilots to an unrecognizable mass of rubble.

Helmut was devastated. Once again, death had snatched another loved one from him. It should have been him that day to fly to their jobsite, not Willie. Had it not been for his situation at home, he would have been the one to go that morning. Willie's wife, Almida was lost and totally incapable of handling anything, including the funeral, so Helmut made all of the arrangements. Struggling with Willie's death, Helmut bought out his share of the business from Almida and threw himself into work. He continued to build their many scattered housing projects for the elderly in Shawano and Steven's Point, Wisconsin, as well as in Kankakee and Joliet, Illinois.

After Willie's death, Helmut was quite shaken and even hesitant to fly again, but he made himself get back in the air and overcome his fear. He did decide it best not to buy another plane and for a while he rented planes when he needed to make a trip for one of his projects. He struggled to manage his company alone and realized what a valuable partner Willie had been. It took this terrible loss for him to understand the important position Willie had held in the company. He also realized that all that he'd lost with his family and his partnership fell directly on his shoulders and he regretted the way he'd been living his life. His guilt was one more emotion that he did his best to shut behind closed doors, but it ate at him and weighed heavily on his mind.

•

Scattered housing meant that Helmut was forced to buy lots throughout the city, spreading these affordable houses for the elderly in diverse neighborhoods. All told the four new projects consisted of over five hundred units. The first three developments went smoothly and were approved by each respective city, however the project in Joliet, Illinois was another matter. To get these developments approved, Helmut had to first invest money to buy the land, hire the architects to design and draw the plans, as well as pay for all the civil engineering for site development that went along with the projects. All in all it was a costly risk to take without guarantee of the final approval for the projects to be built. Once all of the pre-build development had been completed, he was then required to publish the addresses of the proposed low-income houses. When the mayor of Joliet read that one of the properties was the lot located directly next to his high-dollar mansion, he quickly put the kibosh on the permits. It seemed the cat was out of the bag and many other politicians were alerted to the fact that these scattered housing projects were to be built in their neighborhoods as well. The last thing they wanted was for families receiving subsidies, who were allowed to rent them based on a percentage of their meager incomes, to be living right next to them. How dare Helmut try to infiltrate their neighborhoods with undesirables they insisted, despite the fact that they already had approved scattered housing projects as a new type of development. The city quickly shut down Helmut's entire development. This was a tough financial blow to his company since he had already invested an enormous amount of money purchasing the two hundred lots, as well as all the development expenses to ready the houses for submittal to the planning board. Helmut filed a lawsuit against the city, costing him a great deal in legal fees, as well as one hundred days spent in depositions. Four years later the Justice Department finally intervened and forced the City of Joliet to buy the lots and reimburse him for all other expenses. In the end, Helmut actually surfaced from the mess with a small profit, but nothing helped to recoup his valuable time.

Together, Helmut and Willie had also started a two hundred-condo project in Fort Pierce and Helmut continued work on the project throughout the energy crisis. They had taken on a partner named Don Heller to handle the property's sales and it gave Helmut some comfort that he wasn't running such a large project alone. The problem that presented itself, due to the energy crisis, was that most of their buyers should have been coming up from the Miami area, but because gas prices were so high due to a shortage of fuel, no one was traveling. This unexpected snafu made sales tough and he nearly lost the property to the bank. They had not used their usual bank in Miami and the new bank stopped their progress payments and started proceedings to foreclose on the project at a price set below the value of the sales price. It turned out that Florida law did not allow foreclosures below value and the judge refused to allow the bank to take the property from him. This bought them time and Helmut and Don managed to sell all of the remaining units to one buyer at a discounted price and still managed to turn a profit. Luckily, they had already sold nearly seventy units at their original asking price asking price, before the slump in the economy.

•

In 1964, Helmut was eligible for U.S. citizenship, so he proceeded to apply for his, as well as Helga's, naturalization. Helga had immigrated with her family to the U.S., four years earlier than Helmut, however she had never applied for citizenship. First they had to study and pass the naturalization test. After months of studying, they passed the test with flying colors and finally the day came for their swearing-in as American citizens. Finally, Helmut achieved his ultimate dream of legally becoming an American citizen.

•

Again through the '70s numerous Jewish clients and developers such as Sidney Freeman, Ellen Crawford, and the Wasserman Brothers came to Helmut to either hire him, or partner with him on his housing projects. A man named Ronald Grossman decided to invest in Helmut's projects as well as several General Partners in the '70s and '80s when he bought two bank-repossessed projects and combined them into one master partnership. The overwhelming support of the Jewish community always moved Helmut and he continued to be a generous supporter of various Jewish charities.

CHAPTER 16

Troubles with Democracy – The Greatest Losses

1975 – 2016 — Milwaukee, Wisconsin — Cocoa Beach, Florida

H elmut was determined to remain married until all his children had completed their education. He did his best to keep his home life as calm and strife-free as possible, even though Helga's mental and physical heath continued to decline. Eventually, she developed Parkinson's, a disease, which most members of her family had suffered from, except for her brother, Willie.

In late 1975 Helmut received word from Germany about the death of his father, Gustav. He died from a heart attack due to multiple health complications brought on by his excess weight and inactivity. Helmut flew to Germany for the funeral and he and Dieter began the process of bringing Lydia, Dieter, and his wife, Helga, to America. Early the following year, they sold their house in Germany and the three of them immigrated to Pewaukee, Wisconsin. With Helmut's help, they were able to buy a house with a mother-in-law unit for Lydia so that Dieter and Helga could look after her. They knew that residing with Helmut's Helga would never work, since she didn't really get along with anyone in his family. Dieter immediately went to work for Helmut as a concrete finisher and then later struck out on his own as an electrician.

•

In the early eighties, Helmut started a polyurethane company with a man, from Kansas City who had invented a new process. He had found a way to make window frames and doors from polyurethane and Helmut saw how making his own building materials could save his company a great deal of money. He managed to put together several partners who invested in the endeavor, however they still needed more money in-order to expand the factory to mass-produce the these products. Somehow, Donald Trump got word of this potentially lucrative new way to mass-produce windows and doors and he wanted in on this new industry. Trump contacted Helmut to arrange a meeting with two of his representatives and Helmut arranged to meet them at his home in Wisconsin. The morning of the meeting, a young, Chinese man and woman arrived to discuss this new investment. They arranged to travel to a competitor's factory in Chicago to see exactly how their product was being formed. The difference was that Helmut's new formula contained fly ash—the secret ingredient that made the frames non-combustible.   On their way back in the car they presented Helmut with a fifty thousand dollar investment proposal from Trump.   However, there was one major caveat in the terms—Trump insisted on owning fifty-one percent of the company.   As much as he realized that having Donald Trump as a partner would enhance the value of the company, he turned them down refusing to relinquish controlling interest. Ironically, when they returned after leaving samples of their new product in the trunk of the car on a hot day, the heat had melted the frames, making them totally unusable.   Although, they had known the material would not burn, they were unaware that it was totally unstable in extreme heat.   Helmut and his partners immediately dropped the project losing their initial investments and Donald Trump never learned that the product was flawed.

·

By the early seventies, Helmut had become a millionaire, however he was determined to acquire a much larger net-worth before he retired.   He continued developing large projects and all went well with his businesses until U.S. President Ronald Reagan initiated a battle against workers' unions.   Under President Regan in 1981-1982, Congress signed into law a new labor restriction to limit union boycotting, after firing thirteen thousand federal air traffic controllers for boycotting. His confrontation with the Professional Air Traffic Controllers Organization (PATCO) totally undermined the negotiating power of American workers and their labor unions. His dismissal of skilled workers for striking provided an opening for other private employers to follow suit, setting a precedent that no two trades could strike at the same time.

As a result, contractors then hired non-union masons causing Helmut's masonry business to start to fall apart. It seemed everyone had suddenly become skilled masons, thus undercutting true, skilled workers' prices. Helmut had invested heavily in his masons by bringing more than thirty workers from Germany between the late fifties and mid-seventies—sponsoring and training them for work in America. Because Helmut had always pushed his union workers to do the job faster, he had sometimes gotten into trouble with the unions. Everyone was undercutting Helmut's pricing and business was quickly going elsewhere. On one hand, the freedom to hire non-union laborers on his own projects was a bonus, but when it came to his own labor-oriented business it definitely cost him an enormous amount of money. Helmut understood and appreciated both sides of the coin as a freedom to operate one's business under a democratic system. In East Germany, none of his business choices available in America would have even been an option.

At this juncture, Helmut sold the masonry business to his brother-in-law, Fred Treu, who assumed a bank loan and never paid—defaulting on the loan. Helmut eventually paid off the two hundred fifty thousand dollar loan and eighteen months later resold the company. In the meantime, Treu lost two of his other businesses, both union and non-union, as well as multiple houses. Eventually, he filed for bankruptcy.

•

In 1988, the entire Siewert family grieved when they lost their matriarch, Lydia, who died of health complications from poor circulation. She had been the one who showed great strength and courage as she shepherded her children to safety in the bitter, cold winter of 1945 when the Russian Army invaded their home-land. She had seen Helmut and Marlene through horrific dangers, and against all odds, she not only saved them, but kept them all together.

•

Over the years, Helmut had remembered a beautiful young girl, named Linda Nickel, whom he'd met back in 1967. When he met her he was thirty-three years old and she was just a seventeen-year-old high school student still living with her parents, Eugene and Nancy. At that time she was working as a secretary for Hape Manufacturing, a company that made miter boxes. The company had hired Helmut to build an addition to their factory. Helmut had been immediately taken by Linda's smile and he chatted with her whenever he was working onsite. She had a kind, friendly demeanor and Helmut had thought of her often over the years. Years later in 1990, Helmut bought a two hundred-unit unfinished development to complete and turn into rentals. To Helmut's delight, Linda was working as the on-site manager of the property. It seemed that fate had intervened and brought them back together again.

The previous owner of the project had not paid a number of contractors, who still held liens against the building, so Helmut created a partnership with those contractors and, over a fifteen-year period, bought out every note until he eventually owned the entire complex. Linda was divorced with two children and lived in an apartment on the property. She worked for Helmut for years and the two of them became great friends. They made a good team, working extremely well together. Helmut had been true to his word to stay with his children and when his daughter Janet, the youngest, finally graduated from college in 1989, he made the decision to divorce Helga in January of 1990. By October, Helmut had converted two of the units in the building to one larger apartment and he proposed to Linda and married her as soon as his divorce was final.

Linda's parents felt that Helmut was too old for her, since he was the same age as her mother. They opposed the marriage, as did a number of his family members, but Helmut and Linda were in love and no one was going to keep them from finally finding true happiness. The newlyweds moved into their remodeled apartment, along with her two children, David, twelve and, Monica, six years old. The following year, Helmut built his new family a five-bedroom, four-bathroom, stone house in Waukesha, Wisconsin. Linda's son, David, then thirteen years old, worked all summer with Helmut as his helper mixing mortar. From six in the morning until the sun set the boy loyally worked beside Helmut. Whenever David needed a break, he would stop and take a nap in the backseat of the car. It took Helmut six months to build their dream home and before the end of 1993, he had moved in with his new family.

Helmut was happily married with Linda and never felt the need to stray, or to even look at another woman. She was his life partner as well as his business partner—something he'd always longed for in his previous marriage. They traveled throughout the Caribbean, Hawaii, and Mexico, where she climbed the pyramid at Chichen Itza and then too afraid to walk down, crawled down backwards on her belly—Helmut teasing her all the way. They took cruises in the Mediterranean and Italy, but they never went back to Germany together even though Helmut made several trips there to visit friends and family.

Helmut's last trip back was with his son, Jeff, to show him where he'd been born. They rented a car and drove from Vienna to Romania to see his son, Mike's, new Real Estate development and then on to Ublick, where he'd lived as a young child. He even found the lake he used to fish on when he was five. The sight of that lake brought back many fond memories for Helmut of a simpler time before the war had changed everything for his family. It was on this trip that Helmut reconnected with his old friend, Manfred Selber, who had never left East Germany and authored Communist books. Manfred later visited with Helmut in Chicago on his first trip to America.

•

After Helmut's sister, Marlene, divorced Richard, she met and married Glen Krohn. For nearly a decade, Helmut and Linda took short, local trips with Marlene, Glen, and Dieter, enjoying picnics with their boombox. Marlene and Dieter welcomed Linda into the family, as did his sons Jeff and Tom. However his daughter, Janet, and son, Mike, as well as, Helga, Dieter's wife, didn't really accept Linda replacing Helga as his wife. It took years before Janet and Mike warmed up to Linda, but Dieter's wife never approved of Helmut's second marriage, since she was such good friends with his first wife, Helga. As much as it hurt him, Helmut did his best to buffer the rift between his sister-in-law and Linda in an effort to keep the peace for his brother.

•

At this point in his career, Helmut had six hundred eighty remaining rental units and Linda managed all of them and invested in many of the buyouts—giving Helmut the partner in life that he'd always dreamed about. They worked well together since she took great interest and pride in her husband's business, treating the job as if she owned the business herself. She worked as manager for their properties, handled the leases, published office hours, and kept someone on staff for maintenance at all times. Each unit would be fixed immediately upon move-out so that it could be re-rented quickly. Since Helmut knew all the judges in Waukesha County he handled all of the evictions himself—more than four hundred in total over the years—saving nearly two thousand dollars per eviction. Helmut and Linda sold off two hundred of their units and bought out all of their remaining partners.

They loved spending time on the beaches of Florida during the winter months and started traveling to a new area between Jacksonville and Cocoa. On one of their trips down in 2002, they ran into bad weather in Jacksonville and decided to spend the rest of their vacation in Cocoa Beach. They feel in love with the area and bought a small condo just off the beach. Helmut and Linda spent as much of the winter there as possible since Linda had developed COPD and struggled to breathe in the cold winters of Wisconsin.

•

One day while swimming in the pool of the Cocoa Beach condo, Linda cried out from an excruciating pain in her back. Helmut had to help her out of the pool and when painkillers didn't relieve the pain, he rushed her to the emergency room. They diagnosed her pain as a sprained back, however when they went to the emergency room upon their return to Wisconsin, the young intern found that she had broken her back due to stage four bone cancer. He explained that the cancer had spread to many other areas of her body, including her brain, which left them little hope for recovery. Their only hope for treatment would be if they could locate the origin of the cancer and treat it with specific drugs. They saw a cancer specialist in Milwaukee who confirmed the diagnosis, but Helmut still didn't want to believe it. He was devastated as his entire world seemed to have caved in on him. He made the specialist test for the cancer's origin three times, but they were never able to determine what type of cancer it was. The doctors then offered them some hope with a new drug that would potentially give Linda more time, or it could expedite the inevitable. Helmut had always thought that he would go long before Linda since she was much younger and full of life. He felt helpless to do anything to save her but giving her the drug or not was an impossible decision for him to make, so he asked her daughter, Monica, to decide for them. In the end Monica chose not to give her mother the drug, since it was still considered experimental. Suddenly, all the money Helmut had worked so hard to make over the years meant nothing at that moment.

Fourteen days later, on April 23, 2016, Linda died—the last four days of her life spent on morphine in hospice care. Helmut never left her side—sleeping in her room next to her. His granddaughter, Sophia, Jeff's daughter, did everything for Helmut, bringing him food and clothing so that he could spend every precious moment with Linda. Since the dosage of morphine was increased daily, due to her severe pain, it became difficult for Linda to talk. However, Helmut continued to talk to her right up until the end. On occasion she would squeeze his hand acknowledging that she could hear him somewhat assuaging his grief.

"You know I was smitten with you that day many years ago when I first laid eyes on you," Helmut smiled remembering the day as if it were yesterday. "You are the love of my life….I don't know how I can go on without you." Helmut broke down crying as he held her.

When she took her last breath, Helmut felt he had died with her. She passed just eight days short of her sixty-second birthday. His loss was beyond his comprehension and made all of the other hardships he'd faced throughout his life seem trivial. He wondered if this pain was somehow payback for the years he had been unfaithful to Helga. How could fate take this beloved woman away from him so early and so suddenly? Surely he should have been the first to go. Had his actions taken from him the only woman he ever truly loved? Or, had his luck of escaping death in Germany simply caught up with him to collect its debt?

THE END

EPILOGUE

<u>Life In the Time Of COVID – Co-Author's Note</u>

2016 – 2021 — Milwaukee, Wisconsin — Cocoa Beach, Florida

After Linda's funeral, Helmut did his best to get through every day, but his loss was so great that he barely found a reason to go on. Just getting out of bed in the morning was all he could do and there were many times he wished that he had been the one to go first. Linda was so much younger than he and his struggle to make sense of his loss wore on him. His children and grandchildren encouraged him to try to get back to some semblance of his life before Linda's death, but it was difficult to make peace with it. He had survived the Russian invasion, escaped from communism, embraced a new country as his home, built an empire on his own, and raised six children, but he was unable to succeed at the one thing that had been most important to him—saving Linda.

When Helmut traveled down to Florida to visit his brother, Dieter, who now owned a condo in his complex, he found it hard to stay in the unit he had shared with Linda. After a time, he decided to purchase another, larger condo in the area, using the excuse that he needed more space for family when they came to visit.

·

I met Helmut several months after moving to Florida, after living for thirty years in Los Angeles writing books and screenplays. We became immediate friends and I was fascinated by his stories from his childhood—how he participated in Hitler Youth and his great escape from the Russians at such a young age. I found him to be one of the most interesting people I had ever met and the more I learned of how he'd escaped Germany to come to America and his success here, I knew I had to write his story.

When the COVID-19 pandemic hit in 2020, we were about halfway through the book and Helmut found himself stuck in Wisconsin spending most of the summer months there, while the world cloistered itself from the deadly virus. I was in Merritt Island hunkered down in a house I was remodeling and working on his book. Helmut managed to make a short trip back to Florida in October so that we could continue writing his story, then he returned to Wisconsin in time to spend Thanksgiving with family. Just before their gathering, however, his housekeeper came to work feeling a bit under the weather and instead of sanitizing his house, she managed to leave behind the deadly virus, infecting

Helmut with COVID. He spent Thanksgiving in the hospital, where the doctors warned his family members that he had only a fifty percent chance   members to say goodbye, having lost his will to live.

When I received that goodbye call from him saying he'd given up, I said, "Damn it! You were able to escape the Russian Army at ten years old! I want you to fight like you fought to save your life back then! We still have work to do!"

He weakly replied, "We'll see," and I hung up, devastated that he would simply give up fighting.

After weeks of hospitalization and rehab, Helmut managed to pull through, but had to learn to walk all over again. It seemed that neither the Russian Army nor the deadly virus was any match for this strong-willed man.

Knowing that he would then require a caregiver I introduced him to my best friend, Renee from Virginia, who had recently lost her ninety-nine-year old mother, during the time that Helmut was in the hospital fighting for his life. Renee was inconsolable over the loss of her mother and best friend, Ruth, whom she had cared for over the last sixteen years. When Renee flew to Wisconsin to meet Helmut and interview to be his caregiver, they became instant friends and their attraction for one another ran deeper than simply a working relationship. It seems that love can find a person more than once in a lifetime and they are now making plans to spend the rest of their lives together in Florida. I truly believe that Linda played a part in bringing these two lost souls together, hoping that somehow Helmut would once again find the love and companionship he had lost when she left this life.

For me, I couldn't be happier for two of my dearest friends in the world. Who knew when I made the introduction that it would in fact be chalked up to my tally as matchmaker?

AUTHOR'S NOTE

<u>Democracy</u>

I'm proud to be an American. I fought hard, against all odds, to escape a dictatorship, a Communist government, and socialism in Germany after WWII and immigrate to America where I could be the architect of my own life and my future. Having experienced life under Hitler's dictatorship, Russia's communism, and East Germany's socialism, I can honestly say that most Americans today have no concept of the reality of living in a socialist state. It saddens me to see the disparity and division that has festered in this country over the last six years, hearing those, who claim to be loyal patriots of America, scream how America is becoming socialist. Nothing could be farther from the truth.

Americans have been graced with living their lives in a democracy and those who shout the loudest cannot differentiate between providing social services and simple human decency, from socialism. Certainly, every system of government has its issues and faults, as does every administration. However, America's democracy is something to be respected, cherished and protected. If you don't believe this to be true, try the alternative.

•

A birth of new democracy has blossomed across Eastern Europe with the fall of the Soviet Union. Unfortunately, Putin has worked to undermine democracy globally, not only in Eastern Europe. He's even had devastating effects in the West by interfering in other nation's elections, such as the U.S. France, Britain, Germany, Spain, and Italy.

The growing ruthlessness of authoritarian leaders worldwide, who have banned together, has caused a decline in world democracy in the last decade and a half. The lack of pushback from Democratic countries and world leaders could result in a catastrophic destruction of world Democracy, since already only one in five people on the planet currently live in a 'free' country––half of the number fifteen years ago.

The Ukraine invasion by Russia in 2022 could represent a sampling of what the lack of control of anti-democratic behavior could become. Democratic world leaders and our citizens must do more to stand up for Democratic standards and quell the power of leaders who have authoritarian aspirations.

HELMUT SIEWERT

ACKNOWLEDEMENTS

This memory is to acknowledge those who have preceded me—all those unnamed victims who perished during a horrific time in history. I was fortunate enough to survive the horrors of WWII and escape to the free democracy of America.

This is a timely accounting of my past and my present and the uncertain future of mankind. Hopefully, it will serve to inspire others to seek freedom from oppressive regimes and to appreciate what most take for granted in our country.

I'm eternally grateful for the opportunities this country has afforded me after immigrating here in 1954. All of those who I've encountered encouraged me to succeed physically, emotionally and spiritually. A few noteworthy lifelong friends Eckhard, Manfried and Willie helped direct me toward building my goals of securing a solid future for myself and family.

Although I thought my story had reached it's end during my near death experience with Covid in the fall of 2020, a friend told me to fight as I had fought to escape the Russian Army and both times I won the battle against death.

Also, I would like to sincerely thank Cheryl DuBois and my wife Renee, for the love and support and encouragement for me to write my truth.

Current affairs in the Ukraine will have a disastrous effect on the entire world. I appeal to everyone to support the Ukraine government and it's people physically, spiritually and financially.